March of the

Forever Hike

Written by: Michael F. Paul

MARCH OF THE BAND 4

First edition. November 27, 2022.

ISBN: 979-8215425701

Written by Michael F. Paul.

Disclaimer: The following writing is completely fictitious and entirely fabricated by the author and his wild imagination. Names, characters, businesses, historical artifacts, specific places within a town or city, events, and incidents are the products of the author's imagination and are used in a fictitious manner. A liberal creative license was taken in developing a story loosely based on ancient Egyptian artifacts, deities, and mythology. Any resemblance to actual persons, living or dead, or actual events is purely coincidental. So don't sue me!

In loving memory of Michael S. Smith and David G. Smith

Two writers that encouraged me.

For my biggest fan, my son Zacharius Carl River Paul (the boy with four names)

March of the Band 4

Forever Hike

Written by Michael F. Paul

Terrebonne, Oregon

IT'S OFTEN SAID THAT adults should be the example for children. Perhaps it should be said that the young should be the example for the old. Their brutal honesty, innocence, and resiliency should be cherished by all.

"There can be no keener revelation of a society's soul than the way in which it treats its children." — Nelson Mandela, Former President of South Africa

"We worry about what a child will become tomorrow, yet we forget that he is someone today." — Stacia Tauscher, dancer and artist

Preface

Welcome to my first novel. It took me almost 13 years to write this book. I always had a rough idea about this novel that loitered behind walls within my wandering mind. Over a decade ago, I wrote the first chapter, saved it to my computer's hard drive, and then I moved on with my life. I promised myself that one day I would revisit my story and with some consistency I would finish it.

This novel became more important to me as I have become older. Time, losing its patience, no longer becomes benevolent to those who procrastinate as they impatiently wait for a more genial day. At my age, the calendar shows no mercy. It was time to get on with it, and that's exactly what I did. I sat down and wrote. Even with a wife who needed the garbage taken out or a young boy who needed my help on his math homework, I found time to write.

I was always told to write something that I would enjoy reading. So, I really wrote this for myself. If you like this book, that is fantastic; please share with other readers. If you don't care for it, I am still glad that you gave it a chance, and please share that with others.

And this, my friendly readers, is what I wrote about:

Two best friends, after getting into trouble for mistakenly being identified as thieves of an Egyptian artifact during an inaugural comic convention, are sent to a summer camp in the Pacific Northwest Wilderness only to become lost during a day hike with two other strangers. The boys must forge a trusting friendship with two other lost campers in order to escape captivity by two ruthless men who have been hired to retrieve the artifact. Oh, yeah, they also need to find their way back to civilization so they don't starve to death.

Enjoy!

Chapter 1 The Introduction

Jennifer Hart stared out her large bay kitchen window, a coffee mug wrapped in both of her hands, in time to see the locomotive train with its single bright headlight slice through the gray dense fog on the other side of her back fence. The air horn pierced the dark morning air as it approached the nearby intersection and it made her jump. The obnoxious deep bellow of the horn still startled her after all these years. Two short blast this time. It all depended on the engineer. The fence line in her backyard offered little protection to the jarring sound of the rumbling train as it trundled along the rails with its mile long burden. The backyard cedar fence laid about 100 feet from her kitchen. She stared at her dark brown hair and blue eyes in the reflection wondering if time had painted cruel strokes of age to her thin face. The years, infamous for its relentless march forward, had little impact on her attractive looks. Her high cheekbones and dimples, when she smiled, was enough to pause the wanting heart.

Despite the noise the trains made several times a day, she loved the beauty and comfort of her home. She had always loved this small town. The house was quite nice; a souvenir of sorts after Brad left. Once upon a time he too wanted to live in a bedroom community away from the larger cities. Of course, that is when life begins as a fairy tale. He had not minded commuting the 20 minutes to his small law practice in the state capital. A large home of almost 2,500 square feet of living space occupied the apex of the cul-de-sac. The well-manicured landscape, maintained by a hired gardening company, matched all the other homes in her neighborhood. Each home was guarded by tall evergreens, like stoic sentries. The inside was immaculate and maintained with meticulous care. Knick-knacks created clutter and clutter welcomed dust. Jennifer believed less meant more. That's what she told herself anyways. The upstairs bonus room hadn't been furnished since he left. It used to be his media room or as he had called it, "the Man Cave." It was empty now and she couldn't be bothered walking up the stairs unless it needed vacuuming. At least she had the house. Despite the trains that passed through the tiny farming town and directly behind her house, she loved it. Besides, she wouldn't have been able to sell it and buy another house. She grew up in this small little town.

Her fingers, long and thin, wrapped tighter around the large coffee mug she got on her honeymoon; another souvenir from her marriage. She looked again in her backyard and thought about the extended darkness and cold grip that could eat at the souls of the depressed. The Pacific Northwest, with the rain, clouds, and coldness over the long winter took a toll on people. Her fingers tightened a bit more around her coffee mug and looking at the clock she figured she should be on the road to campus so she could find decent parking.

The small farming town Jennifer Hart called home sat just off the I-5 corridor in the mid valley of the Willamette. A few businesses had lingered on. Despite the location, a few new residential areas sprung up. New apartments and cute little townhomes had been built as well. Rolling grass hills were scattered about the outskirts of the tiny town. Cute farmhouses, cattle pastures, sheep pastures, and crop fields occupied most of the land in the outlying areas. The small town welcomed both the poor and the middle class but wealth seemingly was divided by the train tracks that ran directly through. The older homes and the two trailer parks sat on the west side of the tracks. The newer homes that sat perched like raptors on the west hill looked down on the poorer neighborhoods.

The road to Albany was thick with fog and it lingered, just loitering in the path of those commuters with real destinations. That's what Jennifer thought anyways. She didn't mind, however. She enjoyed the drive to Albany. Pastures and farming fields, blanketed with the fog, laid to each side. Perhaps enjoyment was an overstatement. It gave her about 20 minutes to think, reflect, and sometimes dream. 32 years of life and she was finally finishing the first part of her schooling after more than a decade break. She finally had been officially accepted into the nursing program the following fall term. She couldn't quite recall the month she dropped out of the University of Portland. She was pregnant with Jacob and only 20 years old. Thoughts of the past hid in dusty caverns of her mind vying to come up front. She thought of her one good friend, Melissa, who lived on the next block. Melissa was divorced too. Melissa was lucky; she didn't have any children. That's why Rick left, because his wife couldn't bare him offspring. Jennifer felt guilty when she envied her friend. It's always rosier on the other side of the fence. Why do we always want something we can't have?

She had worked out a deal with Brad in order to return to school instead of finding a job. She wanted a career she could be happy with since she was now responsible for a son and herself. Brad had a great career that was quite lucrative. Why couldn't she be afforded one? The details were really worked about between a mediator during the divorce proceedings. She didn't have to work when she was married to Brad. The house was paid for thanks to his well-paying job and a substantial inheritance he received from his late paternal grandfather. Brad, not having a real good leg to stand on, agreed to pay enough alimony and child support for her to return to school and pay the bills. Jennifer would just have to study and raise her son. He would obviously continue to pay the child support until Jacob reached the legal age but he would be allowed to suspend alimony once Jennifer landed her first nursing job.

During that drive, radio turned down low, she also thought of her 12-year-old son and her words that spilled from beyond her lips that morning. Awful words that she would not be able to collect back. She felt that at times she was quite excellent at saying the most horrendous things.

The morning train, the same one that Jennifer saw through her kitchen window, awakened Jacob; the earth trembled and gently rocked the bed he lay in. Troubled by a bad dream and a sleepless night he sat up, yawned, stretched, and then promptly lay back down. His blankets were scattered on the floor and the fitted flannel sheets had slipped off their corners. His lanky frame occupied both ends of the bed. A few more minutes of sleep would be okay. He was ripped from atop of a narrow fence, between slumber and tired consciousness, by the voice of his mother. Figuring his mom would allow him five more minutes of peace, he closed his eyes once more. The door flew open with impending doom and Jennifer, with the coffee mug in hand, flipped on the switch flooding the dirty room with unwelcome light. Several types of skateboards littered the room along with dirty clothes, and a few school books. The walls were covered with posters of comic book characters and movie art both old and new. A few rock and roll band posters were carelessly taped to the wall.

"You're late Jacob! At your age, I would expect some more responsibility," she said. It was never Jake; he didn't allow people to shorten his name. That's what his dad used to call him before he left. Then the words came out of her mouth. Words that cannot be driven back from where they are formed. And with a sliver of sarcasm, eyes narrowed, she stated, "I guess you're as responsible as your dad." She had nothing more to say. Finding the right words to say to him always seemed a bit out of her grasp. She immediately regretted her words and as she fought back tears she turned and left quietly. She had no idea why she said such terrible things. Perhaps the anger she felt at Brad was easy to direct at the boy that bore such a resemblance to him. She knew it was wrong.

Jacob sat there with his long and skinny bare legs hanging over his bed. His thick blonde hair, tangled from his fitful slumber, laid over his bright blue eyes freckled with gold that matched his mother's. He could have easily passed as a young California surfer. He was lucky to have acquired such good looks from both parents. The strong jaw line was from his father. He stood up, yawned, and stretched forcing his scrawny arms into the air. He was almost five foot eight inches, about as tall his mother. He heard the little red Honda's transmission whine as it reversed from their driveway. He stared at his large video game collection and became lost in thought. He thought briefly of his mother's mean remarks.

He thought of his dad but memories of him have become fuzzy and are like chalk marks haphazardly erased from an outdated classroom's green board. It had been some time since his dad left him. Apparently, a blonde client going through her second divorce was more enticing than his present wife and a four-year-old son. That's what his mom tells him. His father just decided not to come around anymore. Brad wouldn't be caught dead in this small crappy town. It was now all beneath him. It was all chewed gum stuck to the soles of his expensive Jimmy Choo's. He had a new family surrounded by affluent friends who threw lavish parties with expensive wine in the west hills of Portland. Jacob had no pictures of him anymore and his mother offered none either. He has been erased from his father's mind too. It seemed this fish got a taste of the new big pond and never decided to swim back.

Jacob stayed mostly to himself. Jennifer made him play basketball and run track for the middle school. He played just to appease her. She wanted him to have more close friends but he was okay with mustering up just one and that was Tyler. He needed to be more outgoing in her mind. He thought maybe she was afraid he would end up living with her forever. He was actually good at basketball and he was a quick runner. He was athletic for his age. Solitude and quiet, however, better suited him. He had many acquaintances at school and he was actually well liked by both peers and his teachers. His imaginative thoughts, his video games, and comic books occupied his mind. He didn't know how to interact with the other kids apart from Tyler.

The kitchen was spotless and the pantry was full. His mother's perfume still hung in the air like a loitering ghost. The stainless-steel double door fridge lacked any pictures or magnets. Jacob, now dressed for school, poured himself some cereal. At least his mom got the good stuff for him. She called it boxed diabetic wonder flakes. The large green plastic salad bowl was perfect for the cereal. He could finish an entire cereal box in just a few days. He had no siblings to contend with and his mother wouldn't touch the stuff. She was too engrossed with healthy food and anything labeled organic. If it was locally grown and farmed in the fertile lands nearby that was a bonus. He sat at the kitchen table thumbing through yesterday's ads. He was looking for the new FPS video game that was due out on Tuesday. He had money saved for the new first-person game. He had waited for almost six months for this game, but it felt a lot longer. It was the second game in the series and it was hyped to be better than the first. He was lost in thought and didn't hear the door. The knock came again followed by the doorbell. It had to be Tyler.

The boy stood in the doorway with his oversized green hoodie and faded jeans. The bottom of the jeans wavered about two inches above the top of his worn-out sneakers. His green sweater, faded from years of existence, had holes here and there. He stood there with his grin and his large brown eyes were bright and friendly. His pudgy face was almost too big for his short body. Jacob towered over him.

Contrary to his mother's belief, they still had a few minutes before their trek to the middle school. Jacob poured his friend some cereal, topped it with milk, and handed him a glass of cranberry juice.

Tyler Jackson was born and raised in North Portland until he was ten; his dad was originally from Tennessee. A few months after his birthday, Tyler and his dad picked up and moved some 65 miles south. They found themselves in this small town. His dad, Jim, found work as a mechanic for a fat farmer who grew corn, grass seed, and mint on 400 acres. The farmer, Clyde Foster, was a short man with a shorter temper that spoke mostly in grunts and poorly understood body language. The farmer lived like a king on top of one of his rolling hills and paid his lone mechanic like a feudal serf. Like Jacob, Tyler had no siblings. Quiet and reserved, Tyler lived in a small shanty on the other side of the railroad tracks a few blocks from the newer subdivision. Tyler and Jacob had been best friends since the former arrived into town. Tyler was a taciturn which Jacob always appreciated. He was kind and intelligent but his thoughts seemed to be always hidden, somewhere deep within his mind. Jacob always thought that Tyler would be a great poker player if he so desired.

"Did you hear about the comic con they are holding at the state fairgrounds this spring?" asked Jacob, sugared cereal still in his mouth.

"No," replied Tyler. He never offered any superfluous answers or long-winded commentary. Tyler, needless to say, was always to the point.

Jacob had seen the flyer at the corner market. The other day he had some extra money so he thought he would take a small jaunt to the only grocery store in town. He had an extra five dollars in cash burning a large hole in his pocket. A large wooden cork board hung askew under the awning of the grocery store. It was obvious that it wasn't monitored by anybody associated with the store. Some of the flyers were outdated by months, one was outdated by a year. Other flyers, obviously discolored, had been faded by the weather and time. Next to the advertisements about daycare and several flyers about lost pets he had found it. It was like this shiny piece of paper haphazardly stuck between other frivolous notices and notes. To him it was a crisp dollar bill, that elusive golden ticket, found on a dirty sidewalk of a forgotten town. He was incredulous at first wondering what a nice flyer like that was doing in such a small little dingy farming town. When he saw that the month of May was printed on it, he was certain that it was for the previous year. He looked again and noticed that it was for this year, this spring! It was a comic convention, the first one to be held in the heart of the Willamette Valley. He looked at it several times ensuring his eyes hadn't deceived him. He had always wanted to attend a comic con. The greatest part was that, the best action actor, Ethan Flynn was supposed to be there. He had hurried home and confirmed it on their website. He explained this all to Tyler.

Ethan Flynn was probably the biggest star in Hollywood and just finished the third movie installment of Forced Renegade. Forced Renegade, a muscle bound superhuman, was an anti-hero that enjoyed the benefits and fruits of his vengeful escapades. Forced Renegade was the best superhero in Jacob's mind. He had collected every Renegade comic book. And so, he about lost it when Hollywood decided to turn it into a movie franchise.

"Cost?" asked Tyler.

To which Jacob replied, "it cost $240 to get into the convention, those are VIP tickets by the way. You wanna come with, man?"

Tyler shaking his head replied sheepishly, "Na, dude, you know I can't afford that."

Jacob looked at his best friend and smiled, "Nobody said that you had to pay for anything, I just want to know if you want to hang out that day."

Tyler looked at him, his forehead lines were scrunched together. It almost looked as if he was in pain. He was obviously mulling this over in his head.

Jacob just smiled. His bright blue eyes had a way of soothing people even the most stubborn. He could sell heated blankets to lost hikers in Death Valley if he needed.

With that they were off to school. They were too cool to ride the bus at their age. They walked the mile to the middle school in silence. The cold air cut in their lungs like little daggers poking down past their throats. They could taste the moisture in the air. The fog still hugging the ground, they hurried their pace.

They walked north along the main road that brought cars through the little town. Older homes built in the 1920s lined either side. Some were well maintained with their big front porches held up by large round columns. Other homes had withered like forgotten plants over several decades of neglect. Over 50 years ago, Interstate 5 linking Salem and Eugene was established which bypassed the state highway that had once carried travelers through this small town. Three gas stations went down to one and four restaurants went down to two. Despite the interstate depriving the town of weary travelers, two new subdivisions were built several years back so people could have a small town feel and maintain a short commute to either Albany or Salem. Most of the small town was cute and well maintained, but other parts felt a bit depressing.

The fog was so thick it was difficult to gauge the distance they had to go. It was a long straight shot to the middle school. Tyler and Jacob were both very quiet as they became lost in their own thoughts. Older homes, some with full wraparound porches, stood to the boys' left and right. The smell of burning wood wafted in the cold air.

The middle school was built in the mid 1930s. Originally it served as the elementary, middle, and high school. They built the high school and the elementary school in the late 1970s to accommodate the growing population. The middle school stood on the corner of the main highway into town and a road that took travelers to the west. It was a dingy gray building that had seen better days. It was a large square building resembling a small prison with dingy gray paint, it was just missing barbed wire fencing. It housed the cafeteria, gym, and the classrooms. Jennifer had gone to this school as well. It was just as cold and smelly as when she had attended. Discolored green linoleum tile, freckled with white, laid between the yellow walls along the hallways. Jacob often imagined what it would be like to grow a second tongue from drinking the water out of the school's fountain.

They arrived a few minutes early only to be accosted by the hallowed captain of every school sport in the hallway. He was the jocks of jocks. Jacob preferred to think of him as king of nimrods.

"Are you doing track this spring, Hart? Or have you been too busy playing useless video games with the moron squad," said Todd Foster with a quick and a not so friendly glance towards Tyler. He wasn't quite finished with Jacob. Jacob could only assume that he loved to hear himself talk. Todd was the cool kid at school. He was tall and athletic and the entire school, apart from the two boys he was with at this very moment, thought he could do no wrong. He dressed like he was from the city, but he had just enough of a cowboy touch to turn the girls' heads. Todd got his good looks and trim physique from his mother. He got his wonderful demeanor and personality from his father, the short fat farmer that Tyler's dad worked for.

Todd didn't let Jacob answer and he continued, "try showing up to practice, Hart. Find some new friends. Try and lose the little poor kid. Why is that a problem? You know, maybe I should just tell the coach that you are quitting." He stood there with a caustic look on his face as if he just bit into a sour piece of fruit. Jacob briefly wished he would have bitten into something awful like arsenic.

"What are you talking about? Which one is a problem, finding new friends or showing up to practice? You are confusing me," Jacob replied with a smirk on his face. His eyes twinkled in the bright hallway as he flipped the blonde hair from his face.

Todd just rolled his eyes, grunted, and promptly strolled off. Jacob and Tyler just stood there for a second and then laughed. The bell rang and Jacob watched Tyler saunter off to his classroom.

Chapter 2 Cleo and a Brush with Gordon Freeman

The winter, with strangling desperation, hung on through April and continued to hurl wind and sling cold rain throughout the Willamette Valley. Jacob sometimes didn't like those early walks to school as the rain came in sideways stinging his exposed face. As usual, Tyler never complained. He would just silently walk next to Jacob and listen to him talk about video games and comic books. Sometimes, they would just make their journey in complete silence. They were desperately waiting for spring to arrive.

The month of May was able to pry the tight grip of cold wet weather from the valley. With the wind remaining, the rain dissipated. It rained now and again but thankfully the coldness had finally disappeared. The farming fields were soddened from the rains and the tractors left mud on the main road through their community. At least the air was fresh.

Silence among the two occupants had settled within the house. Jennifer, as it seemed, became more wrapped up in schooling. She acknowledged her son with a "hello" and "hope school is going well." That was the extent of their cursory conversations. Jacob did his assigned chores that included cleaning the hallway bathroom and taking out the trash. Jennifer and her son barely spoke to each other, each smothered with their own affairs. She wanted to concentrate on getting into the competitive nursing program. He was determined to get into this year's inaugural comic con. She barely looked up from her college textbooks. Dinner more and more seemed to be known as a "Fend;" one had to fend and look after themselves in this house. Jacob found no problems reading the back of prepackaged food. He was also quite adept at pantry grazing. He would make himself something to eat and then quietly slink back to his room. He was a mouse. He stayed locked up in his room playing video games or reading comic books. Tyler would come over every now and then and they would play and hang out inside. Jacob enjoyed showing him older action movies from his large DVD collection.

Jennifer would look at Jacob and not say anything. Words were formed in her head but they disappeared before they could roll off her tongue. The connection was gone. She couldn't remember when it had left.

There wasn't need for a lot of homework. For the most part, it was accomplished at school. Sometimes he would have homework that he had to complete outside class, but he waited until the very last moment to get it done. He had a dead period that gave him time to catch up. Jacob didn't have a lot of problems with schooling. He caught on to things quite quickly. He enjoyed math and science. It was very rare if he ever got into any trouble.

Jacob had managed to save $200 for the convention. He had a small savings from his allowance and birthday money from relatives. He just needed $280 more. He was afraid to ask his mom for help. She would probably say no anyhow. School was her priority, his school and her college. She didn't understand his passion for comic books or movies. She thought that video games, comic books, movies, and the like were a waste of time depleting and rotting any remaining brain cells belonging to a child's growing mind. The convention was only a week away. He instead asked his mother if Tyler and he could get a ride to Salem to go to the mall and then watch a movie the following Saturday.

An old rusty tin laid behind several jars of pickles and peaches inside the pantry. It was about the size of a small shoebox. It had several flowery designs stamped on it that had since faded. It had been there for years and it was passed down from Jennifer's aunt. Why it wasn't placed in his mom's room was beyond Jacob. Jacob had always known the contents. He was desperate. Inside was wadded up money. There was well over $500 in it. All different denominations to include numerous two dollar bills that Jennifer's grandmother gave to her over many birthdays. It was Friday evening and there was no time to wait to get extra cash needed for him and his friend. He also needed extra spending cash for souvenirs and food. Without thinking too much or talking himself out of it, he grabbed every bill out of that tin. He stuffed it all in both of his front pockets.

The much-anticipated weekend had finally arrived for Jacob. The sun lazily rose above the eastern horizon climbing above the Christmas tree farm on the hill above their house spilling warm light across the small town. The birds had seemed to multiply and they chirped their morning songs letting residents know that spring had indeed finally arrived. His mother still lay in bed, a duvet tightly pulled over her head to block the outside light that was beginning to bleed into the master bedroom. A distant rooster cried loudly dispelling any ideas of returning to sleep.

Tyler arrived early and he ate breakfast with his friend. They sat in silence as they enjoyed cereal. Jennifer came into the kitchen and offered to make eggs as well for the big day. Tyler politely said no thank you. Jennifer tried to make small talk asking if they needed any money for the movie. Jacob, with a sense of overwhelming guilt, said no and that they would be fine. They didn't need any more money. The movie didn't start until after one o'clock, but Jacob had convinced his mom to drop them off early so they could look around at the mall. He promised to text when they were finished and ready to come home. Jacob was wearing his Forced Renegade shirt. Jennifer was convinced that they were going to see the latest film starring "Ethan-Something-or-Rather." Maybe the star's name was Michael Finn, she never bothered to keep track. She had finals to worry about.

She remarked in more of statement than a question, "I am still not sure why you guys can't see this film in Albany."

Jacob replied, "this film will be better at the one in Salem, it's a new theater, plus it's part of the mall." Jennifer couldn't understand how a movie is better in one theater than at another, but she no longer felt it was necessary to pursue the conversation. She also didn't understand why they needed backpacks. She supposed that all pre-teens and teenagers liked to have backpacks, and like cell phones, it was a required accessory. Perhaps it was like a comfort item. She didn't even know if they allowed backpacks in the movie theater.

They piled in the car and she took the boys north along I-5 to the state capital; a short 20-minute drive. Salem is argued to be the second largest city in Oregon. It's always running in pace with Eugene for the second populace town. A nice sized town, it's divided east and west by the Willamette River. There were some great established neighborhoods in the city, the most prestigious ones were perched like castles in the west and south hills. Blue collar workers, white collar people, college students, and former guests of the state prisons all called Salem home. It wasn't a bad city actually, but Jennifer had always turned her nose up to it calling the majority of it crappy. She mostly detested it because Brad, at one time, was spawned somewhere in the bowels of this town.

The large mall sat along Lancaster Drive occupying a significant amount of land. This particular road had always been one of the busiest roads in Salem. The mall contained many stores along with a recently constructed movie theater. The boys were dropped off a few minutes past nine that morning. Much to their disappointment, the mall wouldn't be open for another hour. They planned to walk directly through it and then go out the rear entrance. They walked towards the theater and skirted around the backside of it. Hopefully, Jacob's mother left and didn't see them trying to go inside.

Jennifer thought about going into the mall, not to spy on her son and his friend, but to get a new outfit for school. She thought the parking lot was rather empty. After sitting in the parking lot for a few long moments, she changed her mind and put her Honda into gear. Jennifer instead thought it would be a good day to stock up at the bigger grocery stores in the State Capital and drove down Center Street that paralleled the side of the mall. There was also a few natural grocery stores in the area she could check out.

Jacob and Tyler were walking the same street Jennifer was driving on. They were heading west trying to make good time. The fairgrounds were still several blocks from their present location. The weather wasn't bad, thought Jacob, so it would be a nice spring walk through the older neighborhoods of Salem.

Tyler turned around just in time to see the familiar red Honda coming up the road. "Is that your mom's car?" Asked Tyler.

"Oh no!" Jacob replied after jerking his head around to confirm the car was in fact his mother's. He quickly grabbed Tyler by his shirt and drove themselves onto the hard ground behind some boxwoods. Their young bodies prevented them from suffering more serious injuries due to the concrete they landed on so roughly.

As the car went out of sight, Jacob and Tyler dusted themselves off. Jacob had second thoughts and wished he would have been truthful with his mother. He didn't understand why he had gone through such lengths to be deceptive. He could have easily told her about his intentions of going to a comic con; after all he had never been to one. Perhaps if he had only spoken to her more instead of ruminating in the constant silence. He could have just as easily asked her to take them to the fairgrounds off of 17th Street. He would have probably still left the part out about the cost of the VIP tickets. Maybe he liked the idea of being a bit subversive, almost James Bond like. He was sure that Forced

Renegade, the tough guy who was very ruthless, would have done the same thing at his age.

After several blocks of walking, they finally came to the state fairgrounds and found the main entrance where a long line had already formed. People from all walks of life and many in costumes waited patiently to get their tickets. It seemed to be quite a turnout for this town's first comic convention. Jacob and Tyler felt a tad underdressed. Either way, Jacob was very excited and he and his quiet friend waited patiently in line. It was entertaining to see so many people and the different outfits. People really did go all in when getting in costume. It was more entertaining than Halloween. Jacob wasn't the type to do cosplay (or costume play to the uninitiated) himself but he didn't object to see other people participating. He would be too embarrassed to walk around in a costume. Some of the costumes seemed like exact replicas of the ones found in the movies. They saw several aliens, hundreds of superheroes, comic book bad guys, and countless costumes they didn't recognize. This was a surprise to Jacob as he was under the impression that he knew all characters known to mankind. Presently, they were standing behind a seven-foot brownish furry creature that hailed from the planet Kashyyyk. Jacob thought to himself that if you are of that height, you should definitely play basketball or dress in cosplay as an extraordinary tall fictional character that hailed from a faraway world.

After several minutes of standing in line, they finally made it to the ticket booth and Jacob forked over the money. It took him awhile to count out all the required funds. The elderly lady who took the money and carefully counted the cash remarked on how two-dollar bills are difficult to find. She told Jacob that she saves them and puts them in birthday card for her oldest grandson. Jacob had no reply so he just smiled. They both received their neck lanyard VIP badge. Jacob felt very important as he placed the shiny and colorful laminated badge around his neck. He ceremoniously placed the other lanyard and badge around Tyler's neck. There would be no roadblocks today. They were practically celebrities with the premium passes. He and his buddy had access to everything. This was a dream. Their only dilemma was where to begin.

As they entered the second gate to show the security people their badges, they were each handed a nice sized gift bag made out of canvas. It had the Forced Renegade logo stitched on the side. On the other side of bag, it had a picture of Ethan Flynn. It was called the Renegade Swag Bag. It contained mostly comic books. There were a few Forced Renegade figures and other comic book paraphernalia inside. This was exclusive for VIP attendees. Besides the cool bag, they would also have free access to an arcade area. Jacob did have the schedule and he knew that Ethan would be doing his panel with his co-stars at one-thirty. Their badges would also allow them free pictures with the famous actor shortly after the panel. Their badges would have got them an exclusive sneak peek the day before and one extra day on Sunday, but Jacob felt he had pushed the envelope far enough.

The entire convention took up two large buildings within the 150 plus acre fairground. There must have been thousands of people at this venue Jacob thought to himself as they went into the first large building named the Jackman-Long. A mass throng of people, many wearing their prized costumes, meandered around. Jacob was trying to remember if he had ever seen so many people at one place. Booths were everywhere and anything comic or game related was bound to be in this building. Comic books, science fiction memorabilia, movie posters, and life size cutouts were everywhere. There were rows upon rows of booths manned by vendors.

Jacob did have extra cash for Tyler and himself if they decided to purchase any souvenirs. They milled about for hours and was able to get some of their comic books signed by the cartoonist who had created some of the best characters in the fictional universe. Tyler's modest collection of comic books were mostly donated to him by Jacob. They even got their pictures taken with some of the comic book writers.

It was the people watching that mostly intrigued Jacob. They walked by a tall Master Chief. The outfit was movie quality, not some polyester gimmicky costume purchased at half price from the back section of a thrift shop or Halloween store. No, this Halo character had forked over some serious money to walk around in that realistic uniform. A very attractive Harley Quinn and a handsome looking Joker with dyed green hair walked past them. The Joker was pushing a rather large black stroller with a toddler in it who was dressed as the Dark Knight. Jacob found the courage to ask some of the better dressed cos-players if they could get his picture taken with them. One of his favorites was a female in a shiny leather outfit, with black wild hair, and a painted white face. She was dressed as Edward Scissorhands and she was happy to have her picture taken with the two boys. They also got their picture taken with a few scary clowns.

Jacob did most of the talking as they went up to the booths. If Tyler was enjoying his time, he was very good at concealing it. They found Spurned Comic Books, a small subsidiary of the famed Leaky Ink Publications, at one of the booths. They were a small-scale comic book publication out of Seattle. SCB, currently, was known only to an esoteric audience, Jacob being one of them. He happened to have their first publication entitled "The Death of Radioactive Rick." Jacob was curious as to why this Rick guy would die in their first issued comic book, so he remembers clearly making that purchase a few years back. The cartoonist was only too happy to sign it and thought it was pretty cool to have such a young kid own their first edition. The author had another first issue and signed it for Tyler giving it to him for free. Tyler for the first time actually beamed with pride as he was handed the comic book. He never had a first edition of anything nor anything brand new. His shoes and most of his clothing were from the area thrift stores.

After several tours around ensuring they saw everything, they decided to venture to the other building. The second building held the panel rooms, food courts, a few more comic book booths, and a giant video arcade area. It also held several photography areas where fans could have their picture taken with their favorite celebrities.

Tyler was curious about a blue looking phone booth in one of the areas. Jacob replied with authority, "that, my friend, is a TARDIS." Tyler had no follow up questions because he simply replied with raised eyebrows, pursed lips, and a knowing nod.

After stopping for some food and drinks, they went to find the panel room. This is where there would be a panel of celebrities that did a question-and-answer session with their fans. Forced Renegade posters were haphazardly placed on the entry doors. They wanted to get there early so they could get good seats. It was a pretty large panel conference room. A large long press-type conference table, with a black fabric covering the top of it, was placed at the far end of the room. Microphones jutted out of the table. Large leather chairs were placed behind the table obviously for the famous personalities. More posters of Forced Renegade were plastered on the wall behind the table along with large portrait posters of the actors. The friend's early arrival inside the panel room along with their VIP badges got them at the first row of seating. They were directly middle front, the best seats in the house. The first three rows had comfortable chairs and as the seating progressed towards the rear of the panel room the chairs became cheaper. It was like the venue staff ran out of money and or good seating options. The back rows were made up of 1980 era metal folding chairs with the words "Salem Armory" stenciled on them. Jacob now fully understood the meaning of cheap seats.

Jacob was very excited at this point and continued to vomit pointless sentences to his friend who remained reticent. Jacob recounted each movie installment, down to the scene, of Forced Renegade and continued to repeat that it was great of Hollywood to parallel the original comic books. He retold his favorite quotes from the first film. He had to tell him about behind the scenes trivia. Tyler was too benevolent to remind his chatty friend that he had watched every film literally sitting next to him either at home or in the movie theater.

In a matter of twenty minutes, the panel room became a full house. An extremely realistic and frightening looking goblin named Hoggle sat on their left and Ahsoka Tano sat to their right. Jacob had wished he had enough nerve to dress up in something cool. Each seat had been taken up. Those that were not fortunate enough to sit in the hard metal folding chairs were forced to stand on the back wall. A very tall and muscular Tygra from Thundercats stood next to the rear exit. A teenager dressed as Cal Kestis, a young Jedi Padawan, with a blue light saber in hand stood on the other side.

Another ten minutes passed and a large man with a round red face and lacking any evidence of hair on his head or face came through a door from the front of the room. Jacob figured he was more round than tall. He was dressed in a suit and tie. Almost each finger had a large ring on it. One large ring, that fit tightly around his right index finger, was formed into a golden football. It looked very expensive. His face was sullen and beads of sweat had formed on his shiny forehead. It seemed he had very bad news to deliver to the waiting audience. There was a quiet murmur that went across the room. He introduced himself as Vance.

A hush swept across the filled room as he said with a slow and deliberate speech, "I am sorry to inform each and every one of you..." At this point Jacob's heart fell into the pit of his stomach. This was the whole point of this comic con; to see his favorite actor up close and personal. This can't be happening! He had stolen money from his mother for this!

The man continued, "that I have been entrusted to let you know," followed by a long pause for dramatic effect and then quickly stated, "that I am opening up the panel for the actors of Forced Renegade. Yes, I have been asked to warm up the audience. You, my patient friends, ARE in the right spot!" A sigh of relief fell across the room with sniggers scattered about. He continued with his opening monologue giving a biography of each actor that was about to appear. Jokes were littered here in there into his speech that drew laughter.

After each biographical introduction the respective actor stepped into the room and found their assigned seating behind the table. Each introduction and subsequent seating was followed by a long drawn-out applause. Ethan Flynn garnered most of the fanfare and he was seated in the center directly in front of his favorite fan. A total of five actors from the film sat in front of Jacob to include Forced Renegades arch nemesis Charlie Parker. Charlie Parker was played by Natalie Hollingsworth, a model turned actress, who hailed from New Zealand. The other three supporting actors were from America. Jacob only recognized them from the Forced Renegade franchise.

Ethan Flynn, English, was born and raised in Bury St. Edmunds in the county of Suffolk. His given name was Carl Winker but his name didn't have the captivation that the theatric and film industry demanded. Besides his name was an unfortunate attraction for gutter minded school children who enjoyed adding a carnal twist to his surname. Ethan went on to attend at the prestigious Royal Academy of Dramatic Art in London. He did some BBC sitcoms, a few small parts in soap operas, and a few British films. Then getting enough television and film appearances to add to his growing resume, he found enough nerve and leapt across the pond to take his chance in Hollywood. With great acting skills and his chiseled face, he had little problem breaking into the tight circle of America's show business scene. After a few commercials for a well-known insurance company, he was cast as the leading actor in Forced Renegade. The producers and casting director felt that he would do well as the leading man. Prior to filming, Ethan had never picked up a comic book so he was unaware of this particular superhero. The first film was a successful box office hit riding the slipstreams of the other litany of comic book movies.

Both Jacob and Tyler were star struck. Jacob's blue eyes brightened and he couldn't hide his smile as Ethan took his seat directly in front of him. Ethan looked directly at him and smiled. It was hard to describe seeing someone transferred from a large silver screen to a live breathing person sitting a mere eight feet away, maybe seven. This whole experience was remarkable thought Jacob. It was interesting to hear Ethan speak in an English accent. He played a tough guy from South Boston in his films. He was a bit shorter than Jacob had imagined. He had short brown hair with an almost military looking cut. His brown eyes looked almost sad. His jaw and perfect cheek bones looked like they were sculpted. He seemed subdued, but he was very polite as he answered questions from the audience. Each actor spoke to the crowd. Jacob wanted to badly ask a question but he couldn't strike up the nerve to talk. Every time he was about to raise his hand, the palms of his hands started to sweat and he could feel his heartbeat pound against the inside of his chest. Unwanted adrenaline would course this his body. He was perfectly content just watching each actor speak. He became very excited when Ahsoka raised her hand and stood up asking a question directly to Ethan. He didn't remember the question, but he he was excited that someone next to him was speaking to his favorite actor.

The panel lasted a bit longer than an hour. The time had slipped by fast. Questions seemed to wane towards the end indicating the panel had run its course. Jacob never found his courage to ask a question in front of everyone. He was still content having had the opportunity to sit so close to Ethan. He would remember this day forever he thought to himself. He couldn't wait to watch his film. Each actor gave a closing a remark profusely thanking their fanbase ensuring the audience that they surely would have been unemployed without their support for the films.

They stood up all at once and left, waving to the audience as they disappeared through the back door. The departed actors were quickly replaced by Vance. A thought had occurred to Jacob as he watched Vance walked around the room with the microphone in his hand. Jacob remembered going to his great grandparents a lot when his parents were divorcing. His great grandfather, affectionally known as Great Poppy Joe, always made him laugh. When they watched television and some person came on that was less than trustworthy, Great Poppy Joe would say "that man is a snake oil salesman." At that age, Jacob didn't really understand what that meant. Looking at Vance now, with his lack of hair and sweat forming above his brow, Jacob started to understand a little more of what that term meant. Great Poppy Joe had died the year before and all of sudden Jacob missed him more than ever.

Vance told the audience how to get their pictures taken with the celebrities. He also mentioned that the Goddess Seshat had her famous brush on display this year in the big Egyptian booth. They could even meet Cleopatra. He then dismissed the fans.

As the audience cleared out of the panel room, Jacob turned to Tyler and asked, "wonder who this Seshat person is?"

Tyler turned to his friend and replied, "she is one of the many Goddesses in Egypt. There is an old legend that whoever holds her brush will be brought great fortune."

Jacob asked Tyler how he knew so much about ancient Egypt mythology. Tyler said, "my pops says that my mother's ancestors were from Egypt. I guess I wanted to study more about it. I always thought the brush was just a story that was passed on. I seriously doubt it's the real thing. Supposedly the real brush was made out of gold and the bristles were made from feathers belonging to Bennu. Who would bring an ancient priceless artifact to a comic con? It should be in a museum in Egypt. That African country has had enough stuff stolen."

Jacob stared at Tyler with his mouth slightly agape looking a bit puzzled.

Jacob exclaimed, "wait, who are you? You haven't spoken this much...EVER. Plus, you are like this sudden expert on Egypt. Besides, why would anyone brush their hair with feathers?" Jacob was also surprised that Tyler mentioned his mother. Prior to this, Tyler's mother was never brought up in conversation. Jacob never pressed him about his mother either.

Tyler shook his head, briefly closed his eyes, and said with a tinge of exasperation, "the brush was used as a tool to write or paint with. She was the goddess of writing; she wasn't a hair stylist."

Tyler was correct for the most part but he only knew a portion of the brush's history. There was in fact an old rumor that the Forbidden Brush of Seshat, the Book of Thoth, and a cedar box were stolen by an individual back in 1929 or 1930.

Thousands of years ago, shortly before the cedar box was made, the book was taken and thrown at the bottom of the Nile River by a disgruntled vizier who was fired by the king of Egypt. Thoth, the god of text, mathematics, and science, had written many books, but this one, entitled "The Works of the Dead," was his favorite. The actions of the vizier deeply upset Thoth; his greatest work was in a watery tomb. So, with blinding rage, he subsequently had Horus create an awful tempest that killed many people to include the one that had so unscrupulously tossed the book into the river. The storm was so forceful that it threw the tome back onto the banks of the famous river. The strong winds had dried the book which was made from papyrus and bound in goat leather.

The brush, handcrafted by Seshat herself, had been kept by her side. She used it to write and paint with. She was the goddess of writing, measurement, and the ruler of books. One day, out of creative frustration, she threw her brush from the heavens and it landed near the Nile River. The brush was made from gold and wood. The bristles were supposedly made from the feathers of an ancient god. Many believe that the feathers were eventually replaced with sticks and reeds.

Supposedly a pharaoh on a daily walk, with his entire court behind him, found the book and the brush. They both lay on the ground side by side. The pharaoh had a dream that night and he was told that he needed to keep both items together and he was instructed to have a box built so they would never be separated. They would represent a marriage between writing instrument and book.

The box was beautiful by all accounts having been inlayed with ivory and a small statue of a black cat affixed to the top. The outside was perfectly marked in hieroglyphics. Plus, on one side of the box it had a painted woman, supposedly a depiction of Seshat, wearing a headband with horns. The inside of the box was covered in real gold and silk to supposedly offer added protection from the elements. It was to be sealed and could never be opened.

Some experts speculated that the cedar box and its contents were stolen from the sepulcher of a pharaoh. It was of some interest that the thief, who had never been truly identified, was rumored to be an American, and contrary to belief, the items were not in the possession of the British Empire. It didn't stop his Majesty King George the V, however, from sending several curators to the United States to recover the stolen items. After all the British, in their words, were quite keen in adding it to their world-famous museum in London. The Egyptian government also wanted it back and were quite prepared to pay a heavy reward to retrieve all three items back, the box, the brush, and the famous book. They were all priceless artifacts and also according to legend they brought luck, power, creativity, and wisdom to the possessor. According to ancestral story tellers, all three of them, the box, "The Works of the Dead," and the Forbidden Brush, had to be together in order for it to release its magical powers. After all it was an exceptional and magical marriage of items. Contrary to what Tyler had learned, many had speculated that if the items were separated from one another then it potentially caused a curse and in fact didn't bring great fortune.

As the two boys walked out into the larger area towards the roped off arcade area, they saw the photography area set up for Ethan Flynn. It has his life size cutout placed out. The line was quickly forming. They stood in line and waited patiently. Jacob happened to look over and saw a large display area that was decorated with ancient Egyptian items. Two large sphinxes, roughly five feet in height, guarded the entrance into the booth area. Apart from a few missing camels and sand it looked like a miniature Giza. It even appeared that Cleopatra was sitting on a throne within the exhibition area. Not just a statute, but an actual living breathing beautiful queen. The entire enclosed area was spectacular looking and it was beginning to attract a lot of people. A uniformed guard dressed all in dark blue stood next to one of the sphinxes keeping an eye on everyone who entered into the exhibit area.

Jacob had watched plenty of movies with mummies and learned a little about King Tutankhamun in class but he was never enthralled with Ancient Egypt. He had no idea his best friend was into Egypt, artifacts, hieroglyphics, and pharaohs. Nevertheless, he was sort of impressed with the display and the associated stories. He was wondering if the story was true about the brush. He could write some fantastic stories and maybe even write his own comic books if he held that brush in his possession. He would probably have to sell several hundred books in order to pay back his mother and replenish her heirloom money tin. He was lost in thought when the line moved. He and Tyler were up next.

Vance was there and he ushered both Tyler and Jacob into the small picture area. This guy is everywhere, surmised Jacob. Jacob thought the bald man smelled like oranges and body odor. A large Forced Renegade poster was pinned to the back wall. Bright camera lamps on tripods stood cascading light into the area. And there he stood. Ethan Flynn was now in a different outfit than he was in just a few moments ago in the panel room. He was now wearing all black from head to foot. He was wearing Doc Martens, the black boots with the signature yellow stitching. Jacob always wanted a pair. Tyler and Jacob stood to either side of him. Jacob again thought to himself that Ethan wasn't very tall, probably the same height or a little shorter as he. Jacob had always heard that the camera added ten pounds, perhaps it added a few inches as well.

"Alright, mate?" Asked Ethan to Jacob. Jacob didn't know how to respond. He instead smiled. Ethan's English accent again caught him off guard. He was still expecting to hear his tough Boston accent.

"You lads from Salem, then?" Asked Ethan.

Jacob, after a moment that seemed like an eternity, found his voice and said, "Yeah, no, I mean no. We are from a small little town south of here. Can you sign my Forced Renegade comic book, please?"

"Of course, what's your names, then?" asked Ethan and turning to Tyler with a pleasant smile, "you don't say much do ya, mate?"

Tyler true to form just smiled, said nothing, and quickly jabbed his comic book towards Ethan. Jacob told him both their names and profusely thanked him. Ethan quickly scribbled inside both comic books.

The photographer, a short grumpy man with red curly hair and a trident chain wrapped around his thick neck, snapped a few pictures. Both boys stood between the celebrity wearing smiles ear to ear. Jacob was happy that he had his favorite Forced Renegade shirt on. Ethan had his arms around both boys' shoulders. Jacob felt that if he had to die right now, he would be happy having lived only 12 short years. This was phenomenal. After the pictures were taken, they were quickly printed, and the famous actor gladly signed them as well. Vance quickly whisked both boys away. As both boys walked away from the picture area, they heard Ethan say "cheers, lads." They turned and Ethan was already getting ready for the next fan.

"Can you believe that, dude?" asked Jacob shaking Tyler's right shoulder. Jacob was still trembling from the entire ordeal. "That was like the best thing to happen, like ever. I don't know what to do. Man! Okay, wow! Let's go play some video games in the arcade area!"

They quickly found the arcade room, which turned out to be quite a large space. They showed their VIP badge to a staff member to get in. Without a VIP badge, the cost to gain access was $75. It was extremely dark and loud with colored lights flashing here and there. It had a nice 1980 section with Pac-man, Defender, Spy Hunter, and many other retro arcade games. Another section had personal computer games and gaming consoles from the last three decades. There was even a few ski-ball machines and one air hockey table. There were several kids and adults at desks wearing computer headphones and playing multiplayer combat games. Jacob and Tyler milled around looking at the games. Every game was free. They played a few minutes of air hockey and then they grew bored. They decided to leave the arcade. If they wanted to play video games, they could do it in the quiet of their own house.

They walked around and Jacob looked at his phone and realized that they needed to get back to the mall so they could get a ride home. He wanted to stop at the Egyptian booth area before they headed back. They walked between the two sphinxes as the uniformed guard gave them a cursory glance. To Jacobs disappointment, Cleopatra must have had gone on break as she was no longer sitting on the lavish throne.

A middle-aged man stood behind the glass counter. Comic books were displayed behind him on several racks as well as in the glass case. Figures of Egyptian artifacts, death mask replicas, many graphic novels, and miniature mummies were also displayed. Jacob knew that there were comic books about Egyptian history but he didn't know it was this elaborate or prolific. He saw a comic book entitled "The Rise and Revenge of Xerxes." It had a muscular masked king on the front with a long cape that flowed behind him.

The enclosed display area was busy. Many people milled around looking at the different Egyptian items. He saw that the person in the Chewbacca outfit, from earlier, was holding up a paperweight that was in the shape of the Great Pyramid of Giza. Jacob questioned how comfortable it was in that suit. It had to be extremely warm. Whoever it was, the person was a giant. And a warm giant at that. Jacob was in awe of man, standing next to Chewbacca, that looked exactly like Gordon Freeman that was holding onto a portal gun.

The vendor's black greasy hair was parted down the middle. A pencil thin dark mustache sat below his large purple nose. A person, roughly the height of Jacob, dressed as a gothic plague doctor with steam punk accessories had just walked up to the man behind the counter. The doctor was dressed in black. The long trench coat, with storm flaps around the shoulders, formed into sort of a dress as it went to the floor. Any footwear was obscured by the length of the looming coat. A black and gold belt was tight around the waist and two rows of golden buttons that went from the neck ran down the waist. A black round hat adorned with golden steam punk goggles sat upon the head. The entire face was covered with a white long bird beak mask that elongated down. The hands were covered with matching white leather gloves. No skin was revealed in this elaborate ensemble. The doctor held a short staff in the left hand. The costume was elegant, expensive looking, but most of all it was frightening. Jacob was impressed to say the least. A few years ago, he would have avoided this person at all costs. Now he stood in awe and thought it was one of the best costumes of the day.

As both boys stared at the comic books and other trinkets within the glass display, they overheard the conversation between the doctor and the man standing behind the counter. The doctor had his hand on what looked like a round gold paint brush. The brush handle was about the size of a tennis racket handle. It seemed to be made out of both wood and inlaid gold and the hilt was wrapped in old looking leather strips. The bristles were made out of wheat, reeds, and thin sticks. The bristles looked worn and frangible. The bristles were long and they jutted out of the top that curved to one side almost like that of a head of an exotic bird. The base of the bristles was also bound in thin strings. The doctor was flipping it around and around with the free hand, his white glove wrapped around it as the suspicious vendor eyed him closely.

"So, sir, what can you tell me about this brush? Is it authentic?" Asked the man in the mask. Jacob thought the man had an English accent. He smiled to himself as he thought perhaps the British were coming. Another English dude is here in little ol' Salem he thought. The voice was slightly obscured from the mask but he definitely thought he recognized it as a British accent.

The greasy man quickly took the brush back from the costumed man and replied with a heavy Brooklyn accent, "between you and me buddy, I highly doubt it. I mean the gold is authentic but is this an actual Egyptian artifact? No. I mean come on, mac! I would have sold the damn thing long ago. A guy came into my store once and examined it, told me it was a replica," he laughed when he said that and then continued, "I use it as a prop to help sell my comic books and merchandise. Cleopatra doesn't hurt either if you know what I mean."

"Can I ask you, mate, where did you get it?" Inquired the British man. He was still standing there clinging onto his staff. Jacob was intent on hearing every word.

"See, my grandfather was in the Great War. His best Army buddy had this brush with him since he had known him; carried it everywhere. What was that man's name? I think my grand pops said his buddy's nickname in the Army was Fingers or maybe it was Hands, can't remember. Anyhow, this fellow, my grand pop's buddy said the thing always brought him luck. Had it when they landed in Germany. Kept it tucked away in his army rucksack wrapped up in an old piece of cloth. Handed it to my great pops after the poor sap caught a bullet in the chest by the Nazis. Died right there with my grandfather holding his hand. Guess the brush's luck wasn't good that day. My great pops gave it to my dad and he gave it to me several years ago."

"That's all you know 'bout it, then," pressed the English man.

"It didn't come with a letter of authenticity if that's what you want to know. Got into Egyptian history many years ago and got into the comic books and figured if anything this would be a great centerpiece, you know to help with the sales. That's all I know. What I know is what you know," replied the man with a bit of irritation rising in his voice. The irritated vendor continued on, knowing the next question, as if reading the mind of the person behind the bird mask, "and no, it ain't for sale, it's a prop." He quickly placed the brush in a dilapidated shoe box and placed it back under the glass counter.

The dejected costumed man departed the area knowing the conversation would not lead to any other information. Jacob and Tyler continued to look at all the different comic books, many of them were about Egyptian mythology. They saw many books about mummies, gods, and pyramids. Cleopatra had returned to her royal seat this time with a tea-cup poodle in her hand. The greasy man was starting to stare at them with accusations starting to build up in his narrowing eyes and he was about to say something to the two boys, so they both quickly departed the area.

Jacob told Tyler he wanted to purchase a drink for the road before they left the building. Jacob paid for the drinks, handed both over to his friend, and told him he needed to use the bathroom before they started their journey back to the mall.

Jacob completed his restroom duties and when he came back out, he didn't see Tyler. He, instead, witnessed a big commotion near the Egyptian booth. It appeared as if the security guard dressed in blue was wrestling with someone in an oversized fury blue Japanese Kemono Kawaii cat costume. It was a short and very wide cat. The costume completely covered the wearer from head to toe. The cat, with oversized blue eyes, seemed to have the upper hand and it began to pummel the distraught security guard with its oversized pink and white paws. The overwhelmed security guard, now in a supine position, with one free hand was able to pull out his bottle of mace and sprayed it at the face of the cat. His other hand was pinned to the ground by the feline's fury leg. The pepper spray had absolutely no effect on the overgrown cat and instead the mist came back into the face of the poor security guard. People were starting to gather to include the man that ran the Egyptian exhibition. Cleopatra, with purse in one hand and a yelping poodle in her other, bolted from her throne and towards the food court as if she was being chased by killer bees. A sphinx now laid to its side looking quite defeated after being knocked down due to the fray. Jacob frantically looked for Tyler. A few seconds later he saw the plague doctor running out of one of the exits.

Tyler came out of nowhere with the two drinks still in his hand. Giving one drink to Jacob they both gawked at the tumultuous commotion and then proceeded in a quick fashion to make their way to the exit. Many more people had come and the melee was quite out of hand at this point so much that a throng had blocked any attempt to leave the building. People were trying to help both man and cat. Other little skirmishes broke out as people began pushing and shoving. Many more just watched, with their mobile phones clutched in their hands, and filmed the Donnybrook.

"Where did you head off to, man?" Asked Jacob.

Tyler took a sip from his drink and answered dismissively, "sorry, was looking at something."

Several security people with bright yellow shirts arrived and the fight was quickly broken up. Some people quickly scattered from the chaotic scene. Somebody was trying to pour water in the eyes of the battered guard as he sat writhing on the floor. The cat was jumping up and down with its paws thrusting in the air as if to say that it just won a world title match.

The vendor from the Egyptian booth ran out yelling, "hey some jerk stole my brush, it's gone, it's gone! Security!" Other colorful expletives came out of the enraged man has he tried to get the attention of anyone willing to listen.

The greasy man was intent to have security block the doors as he pleaded with them to check everyone who attempted to exit the building. He told them that his prized brush was taken and he was certain it happened while he was attending to the melee outside his display area. His face was red with anger, his purple nose had turned darker, and a lone vein pulsated on his temple as he spoke with security and another man in a suit and tie who had a radio in his hand. The vendor threatened to sue the entire City of Salem if nothing was done to find his most prized possession. The man dressed in the suit and tie, who was most likely a staff supervisor, must have relented as he used his hands to try and placate the seething Brooklyn man. Other security personnel still standing around were directed to each of the exit doors each given an abbreviated detail of what they should be looking for.

A short line of people began their way towards the exit, the same exit Jacob and Tyler were desperately trying to leave from. Two security guards posted at their exit began to search each person to include any baggage they had on their person. Jacob could hear a man in the line grumble to the security guard asking if they had the legal authority to search people. The security guard tried to be pleasant and assured him that the search was perfectly legal as customers and participants of the venue had consented to thorough inspections of person and property when they had entered the fairgrounds. He also added that more information to this minor disclosure could be found on the fine print of their ticket and on the website. Both security guards made quick work of searching and it wasn't too long before Jacob and Tyler had their turn.

Jacob's backpack was searched first. The one guard used a small flashlight to peek around the inside of his backpack. It was a quick search and the security guard handed him back the backpack when he was satisfied that nothing was illegally taken. The security guard then checked his swag bag that he had received upon entering the gates. That too garnered no special attention from the guard.

The second guard was more thorough as he went through Tyler's backpack. He slowly removed every item out of Tyler's backpack in a methodical fashion. Tyler had several signed comic books and a couple action figures. The security guard with a name tag printed Kyle, a tall and overly thin man, pulled out a comic book entitled "The Death of Radioactive Rick." A large yellow and black nuclear radiation symbol was emblazoned down the middle. It was in mint condition.

"Where did you get this comic book, young man?" Asked Kyle with a scowl on his gaunt face.

Tyler replied "the other building."

"Where's the receipt?" Inquired the guard. He kept flipping the comic book over and over as if something would suddenly catch his eye.

Tyler studied the skinny guard. His utility belt barely kept his pants up. Every so often the guard would have to hitch his pants up with his free hand otherwise they would have slipped off his bony hips. Tyler kept looking at his thin face and his nose that was so large that it almost looked like a hook.

"Free," Tyler finally replied.

It was hard for Jacob to see his friend get interrogated by a rent a cop and stated with annoyance. "The vendor gave it to him for free, leave him alone."

The underweight guard conferred with his colleague and it was decided that the two boys would be detained until their supervisor came on scene. The other security guard with an air of superiority held up the radio and said they needed a supervisor and backup to entry and exit point one, they had a possible two-niner. Jacob thought for certain that the security guard just made up that code to sound more authoritative. The security guards then told other people waiting to find another way out as this exit was now closed due to an ongoing investigation. Jacob rolled his eyes. He didn't know if the security guards were being serious or not.

The man with the suit and tie approached with radio in hand and asked, "what's going on, Casey?"

Kyle interjected before Casey had a chance to answer, "this kid has a brand-new comic book with no receipt."

Jacob intervened seething with anger, "this kid is being harassed because of the color of his skin, I don't have a receipt either, take a look! Believe it or not, they actually give out free comic books at these comic cons, it's called marketing and promotion. It's obvious you two still spend time in your mom's basement, you should know a little about nerd stuff and comic conventions."

Neither guard had a chance to answer Jacob's caustic accusations.

"Where are your parents, young man?" Asked the well-dressed supervisor.

"They are not here," responded Jacob. Jacob could feel the anger rising from his chest. This is not how he wanted such a good day to end. A few hours ago, he was on top of the world.

"Call your parents and they can pick you up from the front gate of the fairgrounds," said the supervisor and turning to Casey he said, "escort them to the main entrance and have one of the staff members keep an eye on them until one of their parents arrive. Oh, yeah, one more thing, Casey, please document their names."

"And the comic book?" Asked Kyle turning his head to one side. This security guard obviously didn't want to let this go. The kid was in the wrong, he could just feel it.

The supervisor with annoyance in his voice replied, "I don't care about the comic book, we are looking for a damn brush that belongs to that New York guy."

Jacob had wanted to leave the convention, but he was now upset that they were being escorted from the venue like some sort of common criminals. He wanted to leave when he was ready under his own terms.

As the friends got hauled off by Casey the security guard, they could hear Kyle mutter, "what is so important about a freakin' hair brush?"

Chapter 3 Crime and Punishment

Jacob, walking towards the main entrance, fished out his cell phone and with his hands shaking from both anger and nervousness, called his mother. He didn't say much on the phone other than they needed to be picked up from the state fairground and not the mall and he would explain more on the ride home. Casey handed them off to another venue staff member after recording both of their names in his tiny black notebook. He briefly told the staff member what had transpired and that the two boys weren't allowed back on the premises for the remainder of the convention.

Jennifer must have broken some speeding laws as she arrived to the front entrance in a matter of no time. She jumped out of the car immediately after coming to a quick stop, quickly putting her car in park, and ratcheting the handbrake. She approached the two boys, both standing on either side of the man in the yellow shirt. Her hands were on her hips.

"Are they in trouble?" Demanded Jennifer directing her question towards the staff member.

"Uh, no, ma'am the supervisor just asked that they be escorted off the premises," replied the young convention employee. He looked like he was barely older than the two boys that had been placed under his charge.

"They must be in some sort of trouble if they were asked to leave," pressed Jennifer.

"We are not pressing charges; it's just the young man doesn't have a receipt for a comic book."

Jacob couldn't hold his tongue any longer and spoke up saying each word slowly and emphatically, "it was given to him for free, I have comic books in here with no receipts. They give away comic books here to promote their publications."

Jennifer declared, "get in the car, now" and turned to the staff member and stated, "thank you, young man, I have it from here."

The boys quickly got in the car and Jennifer slammed her car door. With teeth gritted and both hands clinched around the steering wheel as if it was someone's neck, she turned to her son and almost in a whisper, said, "Jacob Charles Allen Hart!"

Jacob never understood why he was given two middle names unless it was for circumstances like this when all four names can be rattled off in wrath at once. He couldn't remember the last time all four names were used together. Either way, he would have been happy given only three names. The fourth was way too much.

She went on, "don't" and with a dramatic pause and a menacing index finger in the air, "do NOT say another word." Her face was flush with her cheeks being the most red.

He had seen his mother angry plenty of times, like the time he broke her flowered vase or when he tracked mud on her freshly cleaned carpets, but this was the worst he had ever remembered her being. He had committed a terrible offense and he had no idea what punishment he would have to face.

Jacob under his breath said, "with you, that should be no problem."

She heard her son, but didn't know how to reply and was too angry to say anything that she would later come to regret.

With awkward silence, she drove the boys back to their hometown. The radio wasn't even on this time. With not so much as a goodbye, she dropped Tyler at his house. Jacob was surprised that she came to a full stop to let him out. Tyler, with his backpack strapped to his shoulder and still carrying his swag bag, raised his free hand and waved it solemnly at his friend not knowing if he would see him outside of class any time soon.

As they settled into the house and Jennifer placed her handbag onto the table she said "okay, tell me everything."

Jacob told her that he took the money to get into the comic convention without ever intending to see the movie. He had this planned for quite some time. He said that he didn't have money for himself and Tyler to attend the convention and he had always wanted to go. He didn't leave anything out, as he didn't see the point of lying anymore and he was ready to accept whatever punishment that would be coming his way.

"How come you never came to me? You could have been honest with me Jacob." Jennifer's hands were trembling.

"It's easier not talking to you," he sullenly replied.

With several moments of silence as Jennifer tried to find her words, she finally said, "You are grounded for the remainder of the school year, no games, no going out, no television, nothing. You go to school and come home. You ride the bus from now on, both there and back. No more walking to school. No hanging out with Tyler. If you are home, your cell phone goes in my bedroom. You will find some way, young man, to repay me and replace those two-dollar bills that your great grandmother gifted to me, God rest her soul."

Jacob tossed his cellphone on the coffee table and with his backpack still strapped to his shoulder he stormed off to his bedroom. Jennifer fell back into the couch, put her face into her hands, and began to cry.

Several weeks went by and school was coming to a close. Jacob and Tyler only saw each other between classes. It was just brief interactions to see how each other was doing. Jacob, as usual, stayed to himself once he got home barely speaking to his mother. Jennifer tried to start conversations with her son but any dialogue was short and perfunctory.

Jacob didn't know what to say to his mother and the truth could be said of Jennifer. They were lost in their own solitary worlds.

Sitting on his bed thumbing through an older comic book one Saturday, a few days before summer break, Jennifer knocked on his door. Without waiting for a reply from Jacob, she walked in with a brochure in her hand.

She slapped the rolled-up brochure on the palm of her free hand and said, "you, my dear son, are going on a two-week summer camp starting June 15th and Tyler is joining you. I already spoke to his dad. One of my instructors recommended this place, she had to make a few calls to get you boys in."

Jacob didn't reply and thought this was just another excuse for his mother to distance herself from him. Without saying anything further, she left the brochure on his dresser.

After she left the room, Jacob got up from his bed and walked over picking up the brochure. On the front page was a picture of two smiling children, a boy and girl, sitting on a canoe in the middle of a green lake surrounded by large evergreens. There was even a fish jumping out of the water next to the canoe. Probably photoshopped decided Jacob. The words "Camp Pertida" were printed on top and Mount Hood National Forest printed below. He opened up the brochure to see more pictures of smiling children doing various activities from swimming, fishing, zip lining, and archery.

Jacob looked at each page and read the contents with a sense of dread. Welcome to Camp Pertida, we are now offering one to two weeks getaways for your child this summer. Your child will explore the forest, go on nature hikes, learn to fish, learn to tie knots, among many other fun, and learning opportunities. This is a co-ed safe environment where your child will learn and grow. Each cabin has entrusted and trained college age counselors who will help guide your child through this wonderful experience. We are excited to have your child in our camp. We ask that campers leave their cell phones at home. More information can be found on our website.

Jacob was not looking forward to the forced group camp. A pit in his stomach began to form and it worked its way up into his chest. He was not excited about hanging out and living with strangers. He tolerated kids at his school, but he never wasted time in becoming overly friendly with any of them. If he was to suffer in this sinister place of the unknown at least he would have his quiet companion with him. This will be a miserable experience he thought as he flung the brochure back on the dresser.

The next few days passed fairly quickly. School for the year had come to a close and that only meant a double edge sword for poor Jacob. He was glad to be finished with seventh grade. He had one more year before he would be a high schooler and one year closer to maybe leaving this small town. There was little fanfare on his last day of school just the normal short day of turning in books and receiving a copy of his final grades. At least his grades were good, therefore not giving any extra ammo to his mother. It was such a small town that there was no point in saying goodbye to any classmates. He was happy to see less of Todd and his annoying presence. The only catch to the trailing edge of the school year was the looming camp his loving mother had signed him up for. He was due to leave in just three days.

Jacob wanted to ask his mother if he would be off restriction after he got back from summer camp. He missed watching television and playing video games with his friend. Jennifer never watched television apart from having it on for the news in the morning for a short snippet of the weather forecast. It was probably turned on for an entire 15 minutes during these times. She detested the television and often told Jacob that it was a waste of money and time. She insisted that it probably destroyed precious braincells with its insidious and driveling programs. The large flat screen television hung silently on the far wall of the living room untouched and only added to the insipid characteristics of their quiet house. Jacob having handed over his cell phone when he was home had no idea what was going on in the real world. He didn't have time to really look at it when he was at school.

On the day before his departure to the detested camp, he woke up hungry and went into the kitchen. It was Friday morning. The television was on. He could hear the weather lady tell the news viewers that intermittent showers were in the forecast and the official start of summer was over a week away. Then he heard the news announcer say, "when we come back after the break more on Ethan Flynn's disappearance." From the kitchen he waited intently on the commercial to be over. He was gutted to hear the television go off.

"You're up early, can I make you some breakfast?" Asked Jennifer as she entered the kitchen and opened the refrigerator. Seeing that her son was pouring cereal she decided to change the subject and then asked, "so, are you excited about summer camp?"

Pouring milk over his sugar laced flakes he replied without looking up, "overly thrilled."

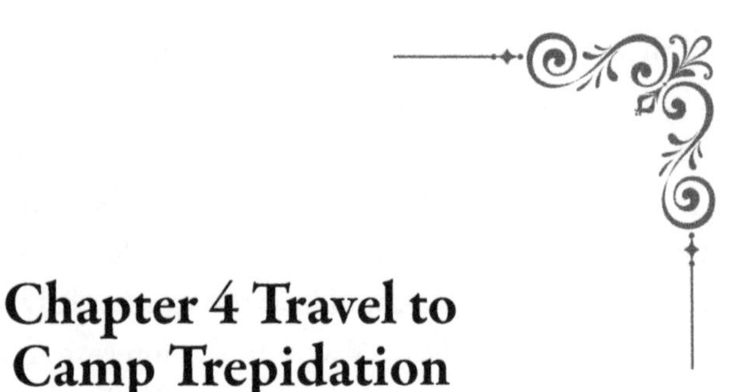

Chapter 4 Travel to Camp Trepidation

Saturday, the 15th of June started early for Jacob. He woke up stretched and showered. This was the day he had been dreading. It was finally here. He had never been to a camp before let alone camped. Yes, he had stayed at hotels, other family member's houses, and occasionally at Tyler's, but he had never stayed in the woods. His mother had never taken him and he was almost certain his dad never took him before the divorce. He didn't know if this would be his last shower for two weeks or not. Jennifer pressed him to hurry up; they still had to pick up Tyler and make it to the camp by noon for check in. She quickly helped him pack clothing, towels, and a personal hygiene bag. As she helped him load his two bags in the car, she assured him that this would be good for him. Jacob didn't have the energy to reply to his mother.

She pulled up to the curb to pick up Tyler. He was already standing outside his house with an old gym bag in one hand and a backpack in his other. Jim, in dirty overalls, was next to him. Jim threw his large arms around his son and kissed him on his forehead. Tyler threw his bags in the car and got in the backseat.

Jim bent over, took his greasy hat off his perspiring head and wrung it in his hands, and speaking to Jennifer in a low southern drawl said, "thank ya, Ms. Jennifer. I don't know how I can repay you, but if you ever need help working on your car or need anything done around the house, you don't hesitate to give me a call now."

Jennifer smiled and replied, "I promise it's not a big deal, besides Jacob needs the company. I don't think I would want him going on his own without knowing someone. This will be good for the both of 'em." With a goodbye wave, she put the car in gear and drove off with the two friends.

Nothing was ever said to Jim about the comic convention. Jennifer thought the world of Tyler and didn't think it was necessary to add any stress to his poor dad. She knew that Tyler had been complicit in the whole comic convention that day, but it was Jacob who had taken the money and lied to her. Besides, Tyler had always been good for Jacob, he filled a void where others never could. Jim and his son had enough to worry about. Jennifer knew they had been through too much. As the saying goes, ignorance is bliss.

The drive up to the mountains was uneventful. They listened to the radio. Jacob was excited to have media back in his life even if it was for a short period. Jennifer had always enjoyed the alternative 90s rock station and she barely turned the dial in her car. Not a lot of words were exchanged as they went through Portland and the city's suburbs. They now headed east and the landscape of suburbia and tiny towns melted into large forested areas with evergreen trees that stretched themselves to the heavens. They had drove through small little mountain towns with funny names like Welches, Zig Zag, and Rhododendron. The straight highway heading east now turned into a two-lane road complete with twisty turns as it meandered up the mountain. Mount Hood was clearly visible with snowpack still settled on her jutting terrain. Bare spots on the bottom part of the dormant volcano were beginning to show as some of the snow had already melted refilling the creeks and rivers as it coursed its way back to the Pacific Ocean. Jennifer loved the mountains and only camped as a small girl. Brad had always promised to take her but his promises were always as solid as warm Jell-O. She silently vowed to take Jacob camping later this summer before she started the fall term. Maybe there was a chance to repair this broken relationship between mother and son.

Several miles past the closed skiing resorts, Jennifer finally found the dirt turn off towards Camp Pertida. She had almost missed it. A small sign with cross oars marked the turn and it stated the main entrance was seven miles further down. The little Honda bounced over gravel and dirt making the seven miles feel like 20. Trepidation began to fill Jacob's stomach again and he wanted to vomit. The bouncy and windy dirt road did little to settle his nausea and nerves.

Tyler sat quietly looking out the window taking all the sights in with a small smile on his face as if he had a hook and string pulling on one side of his mouth. He had not seen so much forest in recent memory. Prior to his small town he now lived in, he was used to dangerous parks, tall buildings stained with gang graffiti, derelict cars, and broken people. This was absolutely beautiful. Tall trees, thick green vegetation, and wild grass lined both sides of the dirt road. He silently wished the whole world could be as tranquil as this.

The trees thinned out a bit and they drove through a large open timbered gate that resembled an entrance to an old cavalry army fort. Above the open split gate, a sign hung on a suspended railroad tie that welcomed all to Camp Pertida. The road turned to asphalt past the wooden threshold and turned into a large circle drive. Several dormitory style long cabins with green tin roofs sat around the large circle drive. They all had matching red wood walls. A larger cabin, two stories, that looked like an elite resort lodge, with massive pillars that held up the wraparound veranda, stood between the other buildings. A sign that stood askew in front of the lodge indicated that it was the administration building. A large pole barn stood near the entrance that stored a tractor and a few riding lawnmowers. Cars parked around the circle were being unpacked and children were saying final goodbyes to their parents. A giant parking area that said "staff only" sat to one side of the cabins.

Jennifer and the boys walked through the double doors of the big lodge. The building was massive. The foyer had a map of the inside; it hung on the side wall with a "you are here" symbol. It housed a gym, cafeteria, a large indoor dayroom, library, a few classrooms, conference rooms, and several administrative offices. Another set of double doors led to an additional open area where several desks had been placed together to act as a temporary reception to in-process the new campers. Each staff member behind the desks all wore the same green collared shirt with Camp Pertida embroidered on it. Each staff member had big friendly smiles.

"Can I get the name of the campers?" Asked one of the staff members, directing her question to Jennifer. The lady seemed in good spirits as she looked at both boys.

After Jennifer gave the names of the two boys. The lady, after perusing several stapled papers, told them that they would be housed in Cabin B. Jennifer had to fill out additional paperwork. It was more paperwork covering liability disclosures. Jacob thought perhaps it was paperwork to relinquish all guardian and parental rights. The lady reminded Jennifer that there was extremely poor cell service, but the boys would call the following Saturday using the office landline to say hello and let them know they were safe. Again, there was no need for cell phones at the camp. Jennifer told her that she need not worry about that. Jacob rolled his eyes. She was also informed by the genial staff lady that a late lunch would be served in about 30 minutes so it was about time to say their goodbyes once they got settled into their cabins.

Jennifer helped the boys with their belongings and walked with them to Cabin B. It was an open dormitory much like a military barracks. It reminded Jacob of a war movie he once saw that began with a very harsh marine boot camp and a mean drill instructor that had very colorful expressions. Two rows of bunkbeds sat on each side of the wide aisle that ran down the middle. Two sets of grey metal wall lockers sat next to each bunkbed. The dark wood walls and flooring made the open bay look dreary. Tiny windows, that were next to each bottom bunk, offered no reprieve to the dark cabin. Each bunk's metal frame had the name of the lodger laminated on a placard. Thankfully, Tyler and Jacob would share the same bunkbed. Children were already unpacking their belongings and putting their items in their assigned wall lockers. Jennifer reached in her bag and pulled out two combination locks handing them to both companions. She gave each boy a hug and held onto Jacob a tad longer trying very hard not to show any emotion. She gave Jacob a kiss on his head and whispered to him that it was only two short weeks. Without waiting for a reply, she promptly walked back towards the cabin door. Jennifer turned her head around at the doorway trying to get one last glimpse of her son and his friend. Tyler smiling, slowly waved goodbye to Jennifer while Jacob turned the other way.

Chapter 5 Milk, Juice, and Nicki

A young college aged lady walked into Cabin B with a clipboard in her hand. She was extremely tall and tan as if she had spent her winter and spring in Bermuda. Her blonde hair was tied up and she was wearing the same green collared polo shirt as the rest of the staff. She was wearing tan cargo shorts, hiking boots, and orange wooly socks that almost touched her knees. Two large hoop earrings swung from each ear. She looked very business-like and Jacob was certain that she would start yelling like some half-deranged drill sergeant. Instead, the young lady introduced herself as Nicki and then smiled showing her bleached white teeth and said she was the camp counselor assigned to this cabin. She said lunch was being served in the main lodge and in the cafeteria, they would find the table marked Cabin B. Each cabin was assigned their own tables in the dining facility. She then told them with enthusiastic cheerfulness that they would be forever known as the Badgers. Nicki went on to say that after lunch they were to all meet back at this very location so they could have introductions, go over the rules, and discuss other housekeeping items.

Tyler and Jacob walked out of the cabin. Nicki smiled and nodded at both boys as they passed her. Another boy, much shorter than Tyler and Jacob, came running after them. He had cowboy boots on, a camouflaged baseball cap, and a western vest.

He called out to the two friends, "wait, wait, let me come with you guys."

The two friends allowed the boy to join. He introduced himself as Josh. The boy, who must have been a year or two younger than the Jacob and Tyler, had to run to keep up as they headed to the main lodge for lunch.

The boys found the large cafeteria within the grand lodge. It was a big dining facility with a long serving line and a giant salad bar. The boys picked up their trays, walked down the serving line, and picked out food. Jacob didn't have much of an appetite but pointed out the meatloaf and potatoes. The hair netted cafeteria workers slapped the food on their plastic trays as they scooted them along the grooved metal countertop. Tyler must have been extra hungry as he also picked out green vegetables and went overboard at the salad bar. Milk, juice, and water were the only beverages offered. Jacob was bummed that no soda would be offered. His mother rarely let him have any sugary drinks.

They found the long table marked Cabin B. It was already beginning to quickly fill with other boys. The three boys sat down together at one end. Jacob picked at his food flattening his meatloaf on his tray with his fork. His stomach felt tight and he didn't believe he would be able to force anything down his throat. He was able to tolerate a little milk just so he could wet his dry mouth.

Josh with his mouth full of mashed potatoes looked up and asked, "so, where are you kids from?"

Jacob answered for both of them telling him the name of the little town south of Salem. He didn't feel like contributing anymore to the conversation. He desperately wanted to go home as he felt out of place. He definitely didn't want to make any new friends.

Josh without being asked proudly said, "I'm from Terrebonne."

Seeing that both of his new found friends wore blank expressions upon their glum faces, he went on as he dipped a piece of his meatloaf in the gravy, and rattled off, "It's in Central Oregon not far from Bend, I live on a big ranch. Anyhow, what did you boys do to get put in here?

I ditched class a few times." The boy chuckled proudly and continued, "pretty sure that's why my dad put me here. I have three horses. My favorite is named Stetson, he's a papered quarter horse. I ride bareback at the rodeo. This is my second stint in this place."

Jacob and Tyler remained silent throughout the new boy's monologue. Tyler continued eating. Josh with a bit of dejection in his voice said, "you guys don't say much."

Two other tables became filled with campers. It was pretty quiet for so many children in the cafeteria. Perhaps the kids were just as excited to be here as Jacob. It appeared that the children ranged in ages from 11 to 13.

All three finished their lunch in silence and headed back to the cabin. The bay was now full of campers. Boys were unpacking their belongings and they were storing them in the assigned lockers. Jacob and Tyler finished unpacking their clothes and put them away in their assigned lockers.

The counselor, Nicki, had all the boys gather at one end. Introductions were made. Jacob counted a total of 12 boys including Tyler and himself. Each boy had to tell everyone their name, where they were from, and what they wanted out of camp. Jacob couldn't really think of a good thing to say of what he wanted out of camp, other than to get camp over with. When it was finally his turn for his introduction, he said that he just wanted to learn about the outdoors. Tyler said pretty much the same thing. Since they were from the same small town a boy wanted to know if they were brothers. Another kid piped up and asked sarcastically, "do they look anything like brothers?" They all laughed. Jacob assured the boy that they were not brothers, but in fact they were just best friends.

After each boy made their introduction, Nicki told them there were three cabins in use for this particular camp. Cabin A housed the remainder of the boys and they were known as the Anacondas. Cabin C held the females and they were called the Cheetahs. Cabin

D and E were not in use for this camping cycle. Lights were out at nine-thirty in the evening and leaving the cabin was strictly prohibited after that. Lights came on at seven-thirty. After lights came on, boys would shower and conduct personal hygiene; showers were not optional. The bathrooms and showers located at one end of the cabin were to be cleaned each morning by eight-fifteen. Cleaning supplies could be found in a utility closet next to the restrooms. Beds were to be made each morning. The bay floors were to be swept clean and any garbage removed and placed in the outside dumpster. The cabin would be inspected while they were eating breakfast.

Breakfast started at 15 minutes past eight, lunch right at noon, and dinner promptly at five-thirty. Other rules were discussed and the daily activities were posted by the door each morning. Nicki called it a training schedule. Jacob thought "training schedule" sounded very military. It was also noted that any violations of any rules or policies would result in immediate expulsion from the camp. Jacob thought about what that kid, Josh, had said during lunch. Were they at a camp or at a juvenile detention facility?

After Nicki's longwinded speech, the boys were given a break for 45 minutes. They were allowed to hang out in the cabin or go to the main lodge and visit the dayroom also known as the common room. They could also visit the gym if they wanted. Until they got a better understanding of the outside areas, they were not allowed to be outside unless they were going from building to building.

Jacob and Tyler quickly left the cabin and took a slow walk to the main lodge. This was their first chance to really talk alone since school let out for the summer. Jacob asked Tyler if he heard about Ethan Flynn's disappearance. Tyler said he didn't know much other than that he went missing shortly after the comic con in Salem. He never returned to Britain nor did he finish his guest appearances to promote his latest film. The tabloids and internet had really been on a frenzy and there were many different speculations on why he instantly disappeared from the public's watchful eye. His publicist, who also happened to be his close friend, pleaded with the public to find him. That's all that Tyler knew.

They found the dayroom inside the main lodge. It was pretty spectacular. A large fireplace, sitting dormant, sat on one side. The room had two pool tables, several ping pong tables, and a lone foosball table. It was furnished with several dark leather chairs and couches. The leather chairs had long backs on them and looked like they were very expensive. The only thing the place was missing were older gentlemen smoking pipes and reading a newspaper. Several children were already playing pool. There was a very long serving bar that was made from oak that was on side of the big room. It had mirrors on the back of it. It looked like all the bottles of alcohol had been put up for the season. A few large screen televisions, now turned off, were hung in the corners. Three very large candle type chandeliers hung from the high ceiling. The dark wood walls and dim lighting emitted by the chandeliers gave the place a very cozy feel.

Jacob and Tyler decided to play table tennis after walking around the room. They found some paddles and some extra ping pong balls.

Jacob was about ready to serve when a kid purposefully bumped into him knocking the little white ball to the ground. The kid, wearing a backwards Yankees cap, was tall and heavy. He was taller than Jacob by a few inches and he was large around the midsection. Brown hair peeked out of his blue hat. There was a jagged scar above his right eye that ran the length of his eyebrow.

The heavyset boy sneered at Jacob, "watch it kid!"

Jacob not wanting any confrontation didn't say anything. He knew bullies were part of life, he figured he would even probably have to deal with those type of jerks into adulthood. He was used to dealing with Todd at school. Todd never physically pushed anyone, instead he enjoyed using caustic remarks to degrade and deride other classmates. He was even successful enough in his verbal antics that he got some students to cry. Jacob had always avoided fights. He wouldn't even know how to defend himself if he was to be confronted with such a violent situation.

Jacob just picked the ball off the ground, rubbed it on his shirt, and served it to his buddy. The boy, seeing that he didn't receive a reaction for his rude behavior, strolled off.

Jacob and Tyler continued their game without interruption. They had no idea how scoring went so they just volleyed the plastic ball back and forth. Tyler was actually pretty good and ended up winning more of the volleys. Tyler was about to serve the ball again when a kind lady came in and announced to the room that they all needed to return to their cabins.

It was a fairly uneventful afternoon. Nicki gave her campers a class on how to properly tie knots. They sat out in front of their cabin, enjoying the nice weather, and each with their own rope learned how to tie different knots and what they could be used for. Jacob had never heard of a clove knot or a bowline. Jacob had trouble with the knots, but after a few tries he thought he was starting to get the hang of it. Tyler seemed like a natural. His laconic friend even helped him out on the half hitch. Even the other children stepped in and helped Jacob out giving him words of encouragement. Jacob was beginning to have fun. He was thankful that the big kid from earlier was another cabin's problem.

They had finished the knot class and were told to head to the cafeteria for the dinner meal. Jacob and Tyler handed in their ropes and headed for the main lodge.

While the kids were learning how to tie a sheepshank knot some 130 miles away, a strange vehicle pulled into Jennifer's front driveway. She had been back for just a short time after her trip to the mountain. Jennifer was having her dinner which consisted of a very bland grilled chicken salad when she heard a car door slam. She peeked through her front door's peephole and saw a tall man with a long shirt and tie approach. It looked like he was wearing expensive clothing. She didn't recognize him and was startled even though she knew the doorbell was set to ring. Apprehensively, she opened the door.

"Can I help you?" Asked Jennifer moving her dark hair from her eyes. Jennifer didn't get a lot of visitors apart from her friend, Melissa, and that was only after she texted or called.

"Hi, is Jacob Hart, home by any chance?" Replied the stranger. His voice was monotone, each word said without inflection, like he was trying to monitor his own speech. He was very tall, over 6 feet 5 inches by Jennifer's estimate. He was lean and muscular. His silk long sleeve shirt protested against his arm muscles and chest muscles.

"Umm, I am sorry, but who is asking?" Jennifer was beginning to become defensive.

"I am a private investigator. Something of value was taken from the comic convention. Your son, I am assuming Jacob is your son, attended that event last month in Salem."

"I was told there were no charges. Besides how valuable can a comic book be?" Jennifer forced a smile. If Jacob had been present, he would have informed her that issue one of a 1939 Superman comic book sold for more than five point three million.

The man trying to keep his composure adjusted the striped tie on his neck. Jennifer noticed sweat stains bleeding through his blue button up long sleeve shirt.

He went on to say, "Alright, he is not in trouble, but he was in the area when the theft took place. I just need to know where he is so I can ask a few questions and get to the bottom of this. Maybe he can help identify the thief. I have been hired by the owner of the item to try and locate it. He's not looking to press charges, I promise, he just wants it back."

Jennifer was far from convinced and was not ready to let this stranger know where her son was. She responded "I am sorry, but exactly who do you work for, you said you are a private investigator, do you have I.D.?"

The man fished his wallet from his back pocket. He flipped open the rather large leather billfold. There was some sort of official looking badge pinned to the inside of his wallet. He took out a business card, also with a shield printed on it, and handed it to her. Printed were the words Bill Paul, private investigator. There was a business phone number under the letters BII printed on it. She didn't see a cell number.

With the man still standing there, she told him to hang on and closed the door. She found her phone on the coffee table and immediately dialed the number on the card. Several rings later a voicemail came on. A pleasant female voice recording said, "hello, you have reached Bright Beacon Investigations, we apologize but we are currently closed. Please leave a detailed message and we will return your phone call as soon as we get back in the office, thank you." Jennifer decided not to leave a message and pressed end on her cell phone.

She opened the door and he was still standing there. More like he was looming there. She looked up to see that a warm shower had started and it was beginning to spit small raindrops on the man standing outside her door. She now noticed that there was another man waiting in the parked black SUV. Jennifer never could identify vehicles by their make and model, but she did recognize that it was an expensive looking four door SUV.

She still wasn't quite convinced of this man's story. "I called your office and left a message."

"Yes," he replied irritated. "It is Saturday, ma'am, our office isn't open. Look, if he is here, I will talk to him with you present. I just need to ask him a few questions. He is not in any kind of trouble. If he is not here, just tell me where he is. It didn't take that much to find his address, so I promise Mrs. Hart, or should I say Ms. Hart, I WILL locate him."

Jennifer caught the threat at the end of his sentence and acquiesced. "Look he isn't here, Mr. Paul. He will be back in two weeks. He is at a summer camp up in the mountains."

"Listen, tell me where he is," his voice became terser, his lips had disappeared, "tell me or perhaps", he pulled out a small notepad from his front pocket and flipping it open said, "a Mr. Jackson can tell me."

"Camp Pertida, it's near Mount Hood," blurted Jennifer. She was angry at herself for saying the place of the camp.

The investigator's face brightened with a friendly grin now painted upon his face. He quickly left towards the waiting car and turned his head back to Jennifer and said, "cheers love."

Jennifer slammed the door and thought the strange man's accent had suddenly changed. She wished she had asked to see his driver's license or some form of picture ID. She quickly searched for the Camp's brochure in the living room. She started to become frantic. She had opened almost every drawer in the house. She finally went into Jacob's bedroom and found it still sitting on the dresser. She dialed the number that was on the back. Of course, no one answered, so she left a message saying it was important. She needed someone to call her back in regards to her son. Wondering what to do next, she put her house back into the state it was prior to the frenetic brochure scavenger hunt. She deeply regretted that she told the strange man where her son was located.

The boys all from Cabin B sat at their assigned cafeteria table for their dinner meal. Jacob feeling a bit better about camp enjoyed his food which consisted of homemade lasagna and warm garlic bread. He even visited the salad bar. He listened to the chatter at the table. The campers getting to know each other better began to banter back and forth.

A camper, named Zach, from their table, fetching a dessert from the salad bar, was suddenly tripped by the same raucous boy who bumped into Jacob earlier. Zach was a tall blonde hair boy with round glasses. He was wearing a Ghostbusters shirt.

The larger boy sneered at Zach and said, "Sorry, four eyes!"

The poor camper went face first into the floor with both hands sprawled forward trying desperately to hold onto his food tray. His cake flipped over and unceremoniously jumped off the plate and plopped onto the floor. A few boys from the other table laughed. Another boy from Jacob's table rushed to his aid and helped pick him up.

An adult counselor from the female cabin gave a stern look at the larger boy to which he replied, "my bad, I didn't see him there." The mischievous boy slowly strolled back to his own table to hear more approving snickers from his fellow cabinmates.

Zach sat down at the table, adjusted his spectacles, and looking in the direction of the camp bully said "that jerk, my friends, is named Ryden."

Josh, seated next to Zach, then leaned forward and in a barely audible whisper and dramatically said, "heard he killed his mom."

Jacob got up and retrieved another piece of cake handing it over to his new camping friend.

There were no mandatory activities scheduled after dinner and so they were free until lights out at the designated time. Some of the boys from their group returned to their assigned cabin to hang out and talk, some children went to the gym to play basketball or volleyball, and others including Jacob and Tyler went back to the dayroom.

Thankfully, the crude boy from Cabin A now known as Ryden wasn't there in the common room so they played without the fear of being accosted. Jacob wanted a table tennis rematch against his buddy. Zach and Josh pulled up some chairs and watched them play.

Chapter 6 Confidence Tower Sunday

Jacob woke up when the overhead lights came on the next morning. His sleep was restless which was usually the situation after staying in a new place. He missed his comfortable bed surrounded by familiar posters and the smell of dirty socks. Nicki walked through the cabin, rhythmically clapping her hands together, telling the boys to quickly get ready for the day. They were going to be very busy. They showered and did the rest of their assigned cleaning before heading to breakfast.

Breakfast was phenomenal. Pancakes, toast, biscuits and gravy, eggs made to order were just some of the foods offered. Jacob filled his tray. Much to Jacob's surprise, Tyler managed to have his tray even more filled. The boys ate in silence.

The boys met back in the cabin after breakfast to see that the daily schedule was updated. Nicki came in to tell them that the cabin and bathroom looked great. She told them to keep up the good work. They were each given a blue collared shirt with a picture of a cartoon badger printed on the front breast. Nicki informed her cabin that this morning they would all use their new knot tying knowledge for the events that were planned for the day.

Nicki led them to their morning event. The confidence course was just a few yards down one of the paths beyond the grassy area behind the main lodge. It was large wide-open area surrounded by tall trees. The boys gathered around the 60-foot wooden wall. It was made from individual horizontal slats that were 20 inches in width. The wall was probably 25 feet wide. Six flights of metal stairs went up the backside of the colossal structure. A final landing sat on top of the wall. Another woman was waiting for them.

The new woman wearing a black baseball cap was now standing next to Nicki. She was tall, thin, and athletic like Nicki with curly black hair. She was in her mid-twenties. She had a diamond stud pierced in her nostril. Both adults were both quietly conferring with each other. The new lady had a shirt that had "Rappel Master" printed on it. Nicki introduced her as Michelle. Michelle was a highly decorated Army veteran and she used to be an instructor at an air assault school at a place called Fort Campbell. It was located in Kentucky. Before that, she served a tour in Afghanistan with an Air Cavalry unit as a helicopter crew chief. She also found time to teach introductory classes of rock climbing during the fall months in Central Oregon. She wasn't a counselor per se, but she was contracted as a technical expert and taught many of the outdoor classes at the camp.

Michelle, going over some of the knots that they learned the night before, showed them how to tie some rappelling hitches. They were introduced to climbing carabiners and they learned how to tie knots through it. They even learned how to fashion a Swiss Seat using ropes. She said it could be used in an emergency for rappelling or used to cross a suspended rope between two trees over a river. If they had time, she would show them how to make a one-rope bridge across two trees and how to cross it without ever touching the ground.

Next to the 60-foot wall was a smaller replica wall that was set at a 65-degree angle. It was probably 15 feet tall. Michelle called it the slant wall. This was used to practice tying off and learning the fundamentals of rappelling. Each boy was fitted with a black nylon rappelling harness, leather gloves, and a helmet. They each got a turn to practice on the smaller wall while a boy practiced belaying.

After the practice, which took a chunk of time out of the morning, the boys were instructed to form a line next to the bottom of the stairs.

Jacob wanted to go first. It wasn't because he was excited about the event, he was terrified of heights. He had to strain his neck to see the top of the wooden tower. He knew if he was somewhere else in line, he would have faked an injury or illness. He wanted to get this ordeal over with. He was very frustrated with his mother for making him come to this camp. He didn't really like his mother at that very moment. His heart was thumping, his hands were sweating inside his issued leather gloves, and his mouth had gone dry, as if someone forced a bunch of cotton down his throat. He couldn't swallow if he tried. He was quite sure that he could not do this. Tyler was right behind him and he must have sensed his apprehension to climbing the dreaded stairs. He whispered in Jacob's ear, "you got this, man."

As Michelle climbed up the stairs, she reminded the boys only one person at a time on the stairs. In a kind voice she told Jacob to get moving. Jacob placed his hand on the railing and began to pull himself up the six flights looking straight ahead. He wanted to puke and his knees were shaking. The rails of the stairs shook with each step he made. He was glad that he had gloves on or else his hands would have slipped on the railing. The boys, standing on the ground, must have understood that there was trepidation with their fellow camper and they began to shout words of encouragement. Jacob wanted to quit, he wanted to run and hide. He certainly remembered not seeing anything about rappelling in that stupid brochure his mom gave him.

He was halfway up at the moment and made the mistake of looking down. He froze and he wanted to scream or at the very least cry. Full fledge panic had currently settled on the front gate of his racing mind. He saw his friend Tyler down there looking up at him with an overwhelming look of optimism on his face. Tyler slowly lifted his right hand giving him a thumbs up. Jacob always felt that Tyler looked up to him. He never wanted to let his buddy down; he wouldn't dream of it. He always talked a big game to his friend, never wanted to show any signs of weakness. This time his friend was literally looking up at him.

Jacob forced a smile and looked out among the tall Douglas Firs. It was now or never. He continued to shake, but somehow pushed himself up the rest of those daunting metal grated steps until he found his way to the top landing fighting every notion to panic.

Michelle, with a smile of encouragement, was there waiting for him and held out her hand to steady him. His knees quivered so much that he thought they would knock into each other. He was almost squatting trying not to be any higher. He reached his trembling hand out to hers. He wanted to just sit down, hold onto something, bury his face into his arms, and never have to move again. She was tied into an eye hook bolted into the landing. She smiled again at Jacob and that made his heart skip. Her kind pretty smile was enough to nudge him forward.

He was close to the ledge. He couldn't bear to look down. Michelle fastened the rope through his rappel harness. The other end was already attached to a carabiner affixed to the landing. He faced her as she coaxed him to go over the precipice. His legs were shaking as he moved back to the top of the wall.

"Look at me," encouraged Michelle. She repeated, "Look at me Jacob. Remember there is only one way down. You need to lean back and trust the rope and harness. I got you."

I have this, Jacob said to himself. He was now in position. His trembling legs almost locked as he stood out facing the soaring wall seated in his harness. He commanded himself not look down instead to just look at the dark wood of the towering wall that was directly in front of him. One part of the rope was now above him and the other one below him held by a belayer standing on the ground. His body was parallel to the wall just a few short feet away. Suddenly a light switch came on and he remembered how to control his decent with his right hand. He had one piece of the rope in each hand. It was time, he said to himself. He simultaneously jumped away from the wall and moved his right hand away from his body allowing him to go down the wall a certain distance. He continued to do this and finally found the courage to look at the ground. He would kick away from the wall, slip down several feet, and his shoes would get replanted against the wooden structure. His camping companions were cheering his name as he slowly descended. He finally landed on solid ground and still rattled from the ordeal he placed his lips on the dirt. The boys disbanded the line they were standing in and gathered around congratulating him. One of the boys clapped on his back and yelled, "that was epic, Dude!" A few others gave him boisterous hugs, one even lifted him off the ground.

Jacob stood up, still quivering, and with an overwhelming sense of accomplishment promptly went behind a tall conifer and threw up his large breakfast. Wiping his mouth, he went back to the tower to belay his friend.

Tyler marched up the stairs with a sense of purpose. His helmet sat a bit skewed from what Jacob could see from the ground. He was at the top of the tower in a matter of moments. Jacob strained his neck looking up with both of his hands on the belay rope. Tyler was coming down like an Army Ranger. Jacob had watched a couple of movies with Army Special forces in them. His buddy landed like a feather.

Each boy got their turn and they were asked if they wanted another turn before lunch. Jacob wanted to go again just to prove to himself that the first time wasn't a dream or fluke. This time he marched up the stairs like his buddy had. He was still trembling and had a death grip on the railing like last time but now his timorousness softened it was replaced with excitement. He felt on top of the world or at least 60 feet above it. He rappelled down without problems looking down the entire way.

Before they were released for lunch, Michelle winked at him, told him she was proud of him, and told him he looked like a professional out there. Jacob didn't know what to say. His face reddened and he could feel the heat rise to his ears. He smiled sheepishly and quickly marched off.

The boys were very chirpy during lunch recounting their events. One of the boys boasted the wall was too short for him. They all laughed. Josh piped up and said they allowed him to do it Aussie style the year before. Jacob couldn't imagine that the adult staff allowed a child to go down a 60-foot tower upside down. Many of them rolled their eyes and laughed. Josh insisted that he wasn't kidding them. After almost 24 hours, they were used to Josh's hyperbole.

After lunch and another 30 minutes of free time they were all led by Nicki to the starting point of the zip lines. The start of the zip line was far beyond the confidence course. It was quite a hike to the top of the hill. They all still had their gloves and helmet as they made their trek. Michelle was there at the summit patiently waiting for them as she finished her lunch which appeared to be carrots and a homemade granola bar.

Most of the boys stood there at the peak of the hill with their hands on their knees trying to catch their breaths. The long hike up the hill didn't seem to affect the two friends as badly as it did the rest of the campers. Tyler who didn't participate in sports was still in pretty good shape. Before their adventures at the comic convention, Tyler would help pace Jacob on runs through their small town. It was a tough hill for Jacob as well, but he didn't want to show his friend that he was winded.

Each boy was fitted with a different type of harness, this one with a rope already affixed with a heavy carabiner at the end. The zip line event had a shorter set of instructions. The rider just had to basically attach their carabiner to a block and tackle type system that rolled across the stretched-out cable that descended downward. The rider was instructed to hold the rope above their head. Nicki demonstrated and went down the cable first. In just a few seconds she disappeared among the trees below.

Once again Jacob was first in line among his camping companions. No other kid seemed to protest. Michelle assisted him in attaching his carabiner to the cable. Michelle gave him a polite shove to get Jacob's momentum going. Jacob, with his feet flailing through mountain air, was now zipping along the cable high above the canopy of evergreens. He was flying and he was picking up speed. He had only been on one roller coaster with his grandfather a few years back. This was the same feeling. It was like his stomach had crawled into his tightening chest. It was terrifying and exhilarating at the same time. It was like both feelings were competing with each other. A deep long yell escaped his mouth and he desperately hoped that lunch wouldn't have the same fate as his breakfast. He held on tight to the rope as he was whipped above and then through the thick forest. The ride was over in a matter of a few short minutes. Nicki with a big smile, camera in hand, was waiting as he came to the end of the cable. She assisted him off the zip line. He was shaking with excitement and wore a grin from ear to ear.

Jacob waited for the rest of his cabin mates. Each one had their own look of terror or enjoyment as they came down the zip line. Tyler looked like he was having a great time. The usual reserved boy had a big grin on his face as he came flying down the cable.

The boys were told that they could come back the following week and do it all over again.

The boys were then led back to the main lodge and into a classroom. The children were given a comprehensive class on outdoor survival. Nicki and Michelle took turns telling the class on how they could survive in the forest if they ever became lost. They discussed filtering water, making a fire, and foraging for food.

They showed a short video on survival where it focused on the wilderness in the Pacific Northwest. It looked like it was produced in in early '80s. Most of the video was grainy plus one of the men, who sported big dirty-blonde feathered hair, was wearing tight brown shorts, that rode up both of his legs, and a faded Kiss shirt. He was the survival expert. It was emphasized on the video that panicking is the number one enemy of people that get lost. It also suggested following a river if a person ever gets lost, but there were dangers associated with it.

Unfortunately, the video suddenly stopped before Jacob could find out what those dangerous were.

The boys were released for dinner and they were told that they would have another short class afterwards.

After another excellent and healthy meal, they went back to the classroom where they were shown one of those survival reality shows. Jacob was happy to see that this video, unlike the earlier one, was made just a few years ago. Jacob's mother cringed every time he said "way back last century in the 19 hundreds."

This video was about a man dropped off somewhere in Africa. He had to find his way back to civilization. The man on the video was squeezing water out of elephant poop to get hydrated. The man, with a thick German accent on the video, tilted his head up with his nose pointed to the sky and squeezed liquid from the manure directly into his open mouth. Jacob was positive that there were no wild elephants roaming freely around in Oregon. If there were, and in the unlikely even he became lost, he would sooner just succumb to dehydration than drink pachyderm dung juice. Jacob desperately hoped he would never have to resort to eating roots or insects either. The video was entertaining though. It was nice to watch the television again even if it wasn't an action movie. Jacob briefly thought about Ethan Flynn.

The boys were told that there would be a large campfire after sunset and quiet hour would be extended until eleven. This would give the kids a chance to meet the other children and the other camp counselors. Somebody asked if they had a choice. Nicki said this was called mandatory fun. They didn't need to stay until eleven but they needed to make an appearance even it was for a half hour. She said that for the most part the cabins are separated for most events and classes. Jacob liked that concept, because the less he saw of Ryden the better.

Chapter 7 The Story of Ol' Snodgrass

The sun disappeared beyond the colossal trees and it was finally swallowed by the western horizon taking the warmth and light with it. Jacob, with his friend, reluctantly went to the campfire. There were actually two large campfires. Chairs were already set up around them. There was an adult at both campfires. One adult had the obligatory guitar. There was a table nearby with marshmallows, graham crackers, and candy bars. There was even hot water for hot chocolate. There was a plastic trash can with long skewers in them.

Tyler and Jacob each took a skewer and a fat marshmallow and sat down next to Nicki. The fire danced and crackled shelling out floating embers into the night sky. The stars seemed so much brighter here thought Jacob as he stuck his marshmallow in tall flame. It immediately turned into a small fireball and slipped off the stick and dropped into the scorching blaze. Nicki got up and returned with her own skewer and showed the boys to hover the marshmallow just above red coals. She warned them to not put them through a flame. After a few moments of carefully rotating the marshmallow, it turned from white to golden brown.

Nicki smiled and said in a very poor French accent, "viola, bien fait!" After letting it cool, she popped it in her mouth. She had a big smile on her as she munched on her golden treat. Jacob silently wished his mother was as half as cool as Nicki.

After a few moments of silence Nicki said, "Jacob, I am quite impressed after this weekend. You seemed very uncomfortable yesterday and today you looked like a natural leader."

Jacob didn't know how to respond. He thought for a second and then replied with a sheepish smile, "huh, thank you. I thought this placed was gunna suck. It's not that bad. Pretty nice accommodations and the food isn't that bad." Jacob was looking around for Michelle.

Nicki told them that the camp was fairly new and it was kept open almost year around. It was open in the summer for children and it offered events to adults during the rest of the year. A lot of different companies had their staff attend for team building exercises. Conferences were also held year around. There were many one room cabins that were used for lodging during the winter months.

More children sat down around their fire. Some children were from other cabins. Jacob even noticed a few girls had sat down next to them. Nicki had a full audience now and she wanted to know if they were ready to hear a scary story. Nobody answered. She poked her stick in the fire moving a log closer to the center. The fire blazed up casting dancing light and shadow against her young face. More embers floated up and disappeared into the cold night.

With a sly smile, she began her story.

Apparently before this camp was built an old cabin occupied this very area. It had been built in the early 1930s. A long time ago that one room cabin housed a very ill-tempered tenant named Silas Snodgrass. He was a skinny old man that always wore the same red coveralls. In fact, remnants of the foundation of the cabin can still be found several yards behind the main lodge. It has since been overgrown with ferns and other underbrush, however, if one looks closely, they can still see the outline of ol' Snodgrass's one room log cabin.

Silas had had an old rusted out pickup that he drove into Sandy to stock up on necessities. The old thing barely ran. Some say it had more rust than paint. It had side steps and an old splintered wood deck for a bed.

The cantankerous old fella spoke very few words on the rare occasion he went to town. The surly old man only replied in grunts and snorts. It was rumored that he fled to the woods after his wife mysteriously died at an early age. He only drove his old truck to Sandy once or twice a year to stock up on the necessaries. Some say he just stopped all together making it to town because his old trusty truck died for good.

A few years before Camp Pertida was built and officially opened, two hikers, a young husband and wife, were doing a section of the Pacific Crest Trail also known as the PCT. They stopped by the mountain town of Rhododendron to pick up something to eat and replenish supplies. Looking haggard and disheveled, the owner of the small store asked if they were okay. He offered them both free coffees.

The hikers told a story that they had accidentally gotten off the trail and found themselves near a cabin with a rusty truck parked outside. This had just happened the evening before they explained to the store keeper. It was getting dark and the cold was starting to set in.

They knocked on the door of that old cabin. They heard a deadbolt being unlocked and a thin old man with a white beard and matching hair opened the door. He had a coveralls on. They hung on him like a giant tent. Behind the man was a small white dog with an awful underbite and crooked teeth. It looked like a Lhasa Apso; the little dogs that originated from Tibet. Supposedly they were bred to act as sentinels for the monasteries located high in the mountains. The man had a fire going.

The hikers politely asked if they could get a ride to town or at least to highway 26. The man seemed grumpy but motioned them to enter his small cabin. The couple repeated their question to the man as they both stepped into his small dingy hovel. He mumbled something in response to which the hikers asked if he could again repeat himself.

The tenant of the cabin with irritation loudly said, "no, truck's broke."

The hikers looked around to see if they could spy a landline. There were no pictures on the wall. There was an old kitchen table, torn couch, and a small bed. The place smelled of cabbage and mildew. The small one room cabin was very warm due to the crackling fire in the wood stove. The wood stove glowed as a black kettle sat on it emitting steam. The only light being emitted was the glow from the fire and the flame from a single lantern. The light danced on the timbered walls making the room eerie.

"Sit," said the man gruffly.

The hikers, now feeling uncomfortable, decided it was time to leave. They deeply wished they hadn't knocked and this cantankerous man's door. They could easily follow the parked truck's path back to the highway. There had to be a vehicle path from the cabin to a road. They hadn't even bothered putting down their backpacks. The wife tried to open the door but it was jammed shut or perhaps it was somehow locked.

"Please let us out," the woman pleaded.

"It's late, you twos can stay. Sun's down now. You both take that bed, I gots the couch. Name's Sirus Snodgrass, my dog here is, he's Goliath. He's a good boy."

The husband convinced his distraught wife that maybe they should stay. It was too dark to travel. They were exhausted and hungry.

Sirus offered them tepid gruel and stale bread which they reluctantly took. The couple shared cold water from a blue tin mug. The old man didn't speak during their meal. He just eyed them with a sour and suspicious frown. The dog didn't look much friendlier.

After their meager meal, the man warned them not to leave that it wasn't safe outside the cabin after dark. He told the couple that he heard on the radio earlier that there was a deranged man that had recently escaped the Clackamas County jail and he was on the loose.

He supposedly had made his way east. Unverified accounts said that he was spotted near Zig Zag that morning.

"He don't sound a like a good man, nobody you want to go messin' with," admonished the crotchety tenant.

The old man turned the lantern off and told the couple they could leave after daybreak. He told them it was time to get some rest. The young wife couldn't sleep. She tossed and turned for several hours with her eyes wide open. She couldn't take it anymore. Hearing the old man snoring on the couch, she shook her husband awake.

"We need to get out of here," whispered the woman, "I don't feel safe. Can't believe his story about the escaped inmate, I don't even see a radio in this shack. I mean, really?! There is something really odd about him." She tilted her head toward the couch as if there was any uncertainty to whom she was talking about.

The husband after very little convincing got up from the bed. She waited for her husband to put on his hiking boots; she never bothered taking hers off. They slowly and quietly grabbed their jackets and backpacks. The old man stopped snoring and the couple froze in their tracks. They both held their breaths. They were afraid to move or make a sound. The old man shifted then sat up and after a few moments, he lay back down. Like an old engine trying to start, he began to sputter, cough, hack, and then went back to snoring. The husband and wife now tip toed to the door and they continued to listen to the old man. He was now grumbling in his sleep. The dog was sleeping next to the fire on an old faded rug. The little furry pet stirred a few times, whined, and pawed at something like it was dreaming, perhaps it was chasing a rabbit.

The pair were now at the threshold of the confining shanty. They were quite certain that he and his four-legged companion were fast asleep. With one foot on the wall, the man used it as leverage to spring the door open. The dog was now awake and began to growl and bark. Grabbing his wife's hand, they ran. With the canopy of trees and cloud cover, they couldn't see anything. It was pitch black outside. They ran squarely into the back of the old pickup. The husband dusted himself off and frantically searched for his flashlight. His hands were shaking as he rummaged through his oversized hiking rucksack. The dog was yapping at the door. For such a small animal it had a vicious sounding growl and bark.

"Stop!" The couple heard the old man yell through the dark. Then he roared, "you twos git back here, now!"

The husband finally found his flashlight and it failed to turn on. He had just replaced the batteries! He slapped it against his hand a few times and it flickered on as if it was somehow protesting.

Using the flashlight, they found the dirt vehicle path. They ran as fast as they could. They could hear the truck trying to turn over. The tired engine cranked and cranked. It fired up and then just as quickly it died.

Their flashlight was failing and was now flickering threatening to turn off. The husband was banging it on his hand as they ran. The woman tripped on a wayward root. The husband stopped and yanked her up.

"Let's go!" The man screamed.

They heard the pickup backfire and it suddenly came to life. They saw the headlights come on and the lights were now beaming through the forest. In front of them on their path, stood what looked like a man. His body was partially lit up from the old truck's headlights. The old lights bled through the trees casting a ghastly shadow on the lone man's face.

"Help us," screamed the distraught wife. "Please!"

As they got closer, they could see the man had a sardonic smile. He had long thin matted hair and a scruffy face. He was wearing blue jeans and a white thermal undershirt. An orange marking was now visible on the chest of his thermal long sleeve shirt.

The couple stopped in their tracks realizing they had just run into the prison escapee. It had to be him. There appeared to be an orange stripe down one of the legs of his blue jeans. Part of his jeans were ripped.

"Where ya two love birds off to? A little late to be romancing," the man said cackling. He brandished a shiny knife.

The couple out of sheer terror couldn't move. They had to do something. He moved closer to the couple still smiling and holding the knife in the air.

The hikers quickly sidled into a tree stand. Before the man could react, the rusty pickup, speeding with a rooster tail of dirt trailing it, sped along and hit the prisoner knocking him several feet into the air. The old truck skidded to a halt and then it abruptly died along with its headlights. It was once again dark apart from the man's flickering flashlight.

The couple didn't bother to see if the prisoner got up. They sprinted for the highway hand in hand. It was several miles on the old beaten path until they found the highway. At the intersection of the dirt road and the highway laid a sign to one side riddled with bullet holes. It read "Pertida Road (Private)." The couple wanted to collapse from pure exhaustion. It was a good thing that they were avid hikers and in pretty decent shape. The couple felt that they were out of danger and they proceeded to walk all night and into the morning until they came to that very store they were now standing in telling their tale.

The weary hikers ended their story to the shopkeeper. At some point during their harrowing tale, a sheriff deputy had stopped in the store to grab refreshments. He had heard the very end of their story.

Drinking freshly poured hot coffee and biting into a donut, he interjected with crumbs spilling from his open mouth. "We caught that escaped nut this morning on the highway. Looked like he got hit by a Mac Truck!" He paused to wipe a few crumbs off his badge. "Boy! Broken arm and abrasions all over his body. Just limpin' along the highway. His prison clothes looked like they went through the wringer. Damn funny sight if you ask me. He actually seemed happy he got caught."

The shopkeeper's face was ashen. It took him a second to digest the story that he just heard. He told the hikers that Sirus Snodgrass died about ten years ago. He was found dead on his bed in that old cabin, still wearing those coveralls. His little dog had died next to him, his snout was on the man's skinny chest. They never did find his rusted-out pickup. The store owner told the couple that if they were talking about the cabin off old Pertida Road, it had been razed several years ago. It had been demolished to accommodate a new camp that was to be built.

Nicki, after finishing her drawn out ghost story, laughed. The kids didn't know how to react. Jacob loved stories. He thought Nicki did a great job telling this one. He wanted to remember it so he could write it down later. Hopefully he could retell the story if he ever went camping again.

Nicki couldn't help herself and said, "okay kids, if you ever get lost stay out of scary looking cabins. Who hasn't seen Cabin in the Woods?"

There was still no reaction. She was the only one smiling. Jacob watched that movie a year ago with Tyler. It was a rated R movie so they waited until Jennifer was asleep before they started it.

"Okay, remember, lights out at eleven. I suggest going to bed early though, we have another big day planned," Nicki added.

Jacob took her advice, so he and his buddy went back to the cabin and fell into their beds well before the lights went out.

Chapter 8 The Morel is Don't Eat Mushrooms

Monday morning came too early thought Jacob. He blinked several times as he tried to adjust his eyes to the overhead lights. He was beginning to have a good time at this place, but he was looking forward to sleeping in late when he returned back home and into his own bed.

It was another good breakfast. This time, the staff had added more packaged goods to the salad bar. He stuffed some granola bars, a package of trail nuts, and a protein bar in his pants. They even had tin cans stacked up. Several cans were labeled Vienna Sausages. He didn't recall ever seeing those in his kitchen pantry. Looking at his tray stacked with bacon, sausages, waffles, and a Denver omelet and also thinking about the accommodations, Jacob began to wonder if his mother had paid a small fortune for him and Tyler to attend this camp. She obviously didn't use any money from her tin can funds.

Jacob sat his in usual spot near the end of the table. The table began to fill up. One of the camp friends asked Jacob where Tyler was.

"That's a good question. Didn't see him after we cleaned the cabin," responded Jacob.

Just as he finished his sentence, Tyler came rushing into the cafeteria. He picked up his food and sat next to his best friend. Jacob asked where he had been.

"Busy, sorry."

Jacob had his mouth full again, this time with crispy bacon, and decided not to press him.

One kid from their table, named Jarod, asked what was on the schedule today. Zach answered, "looks like we are doing wilderness survival this morning. Hands on stuff. Hope they don't make us eat insects."

Josh found his opportunity to speak up, "My uncle's a Green Beret. Had to kill a wild chicken with his bare hands during his training. Tracked it through the forest and snuck up on it and then snapped his neck. Told me he had to eat it raw while it was still twitching," seeing he was getting the doubtful eye from some of his fellow friends he added "it's true, feathers and all."

Jacob desperately wanted to point out that eating raw chicken carried too much risk with the number of bacteria in it. His mother always scrubbed down the entire kitchen with bleach after she prepared it. She bleached it all, even surfaces that the raw chicken hadn't touched. He speculated that all Central Oregon boys were probably a little full of themselves. He had actually grown to like Josh despite his inflated stories. Josh had actually come up and hugged him after he got off that awful rappelling wall. Jacob just smiled and let his new friend finish his story of his chicken killing uncle.

After breakfast, the Badgers from Cabin B were led out on a trail away from the main camp. They were all in a single file line. Michelle was out front and Nicki was trailing the children. Both adults pulling along a rolling plastic storage box. Along the walk, Michelle would point out the different plants naming them. Nicki also offered her flora and fauna expertise. Nicki was a biology major at Oregon State University and was able to name every tree, plant, and forest animal. After college she wanted to work for the department of forestry. She was hoping to one day manage the forest they were now in.

The trail ended and turned into a small open area with wooden kiosk placed around the perimeter. The kiosks had different plants pressed into them by glass with descriptions under them.

"Let's gather around, boys," said Nicki.

Michelle and Nicki took turns explaining the different plants found in the Pacific Northwest, particularly the ones that were found in the Cascades. They pointed to the ones that were edible and also showed the ones that were very poisonous. Michelle put on medical gloves and then reached into a tub she brought along and pulled out a variety of mushrooms.

"These kiddos are obviously fungi. And sometimes kids, they aren't fun guys! Bu-da-dum-dum, I'll be here all week, seriously, it's my schedule, enjoy the prime rib. Okay, tough audience, I see. This one is known as a death cap mushroom AKA Amanita phalloides. Taste delicious from what I understand, but this will start damaging your liver after 'bout six hours. You wouldn't believe how many people have accidentally eaten these thinking they were something you would find in a grocery store."

Nicki interjected, "these little killers are found near certain trees like the birch or filbert. Also, cooking them doesn't neutralize the poison. There are edible ones that you can find in the wild, most notably are the Chanterelle, Boletes, the Morel, and Oysters. The Doug firs you see around actually support the boletes and chanterelles."

Michelle added, "if you are lost in the woods and hungry, I just recommend staying away from mushrooms all together. If you decide to go mushroom hunting make sure you go with an adult who knows how to properly identify the edible kind. You end up eating the wrong mushroom and it could be your last meal."

Jacob thought to himself that there would be no worries there, he couldn't stand mushrooms. He thought they tasted like soft musty meat covered in dirt. He never did care for them and probably never would. He never understood why his mother loved them on her artichoke pizza or on her chicken salads.

Michelle and Nicki then went into a long lecture on other edible roots and wild berries. They brought out examples and showed the boys on what to look for. They showed them edible berries and the non-edible ones. Nicki told them that there were several books in the library they could check out to learn more. They were even allowed to sample some of the edible berries. They tasted bitter. Thankfully, they were not asked to eat insects.

After the lecture, they were each handed a clipboard, paper, and pencil. They were instructed to double up and try to identify different plants along another path. Jacob and Tyler paired up and did the best they could with the knowledge they had just gained. They both thought it was fun. They were learning cool stuff and it was better than being in school. It took them an hour to complete their assignment.

The boys were finally released for lunch.

During their lunch meal, the lodging office asked Nicki to call Jennifer Hart, Jacob's mother.

Jennifer was sitting at home waiting anxiously next to her cell phone. It rang making her jump. She answered. It was the boys' camp counselor, a young lady named Nicki.

Jennifer told Nicki about the encounter with the strange man on Saturday. She was worried that he might be headed up to the mountain to harass her son. She said he was driving a very nice looking black boxy looking SUV. She didn't know what kind of SUV it was.

Nicki told her that there was nothing to worry about. The camp was on private property and strangers were never allowed to interact with any of the children. If there were any issues with unwanted trespassers, the county sheriff or state police would be contacted. Jennifer asked that this conversation be kept private, she didn't want to worry her son. Nicki said that wouldn't be a problem. She told Jennifer that Jacob and Tyler had become her favorite campers. She would have Jacob call the following Saturday to say hello.

After lunch the kids got hands on experience on filtering water from a nearby stream. Michelle showed them a variety of commercial water filters that could be bought at camping and survival stores. She even showed them disinfecting tablets that could be used to kill bacteria in the water. She told them to follow the directions on the packaging.

The campers also got a class on different way to start a campfire. Each child got to have their hand in using different methods to start a fire. Jacob was excited to use sticks as friction to start a small fire. It was pretty neat to learn how to start a fire without matches. They learned how to use the bow drill, pump drill, hand drill, and fire plough. The important thing out of that lesson though was to always have fireproof matches or a survival lighter. Jacob helped Tyler and Zach start their own fires. Nicki warned Jacob to not get too carried away with the fire, he could end up wetting the bed later that night. Jacob didn't understand the reference but laughed anyhow.

After the survival class, the children were released for the evening. The boys all walked together back to the camp and headed for the cafeteria. After dinner they could go into the lodge and they were now allowed outside as long as they stayed close to the cabins.

The entire cabin of boys played outside after dinner. Somebody found an old plastic flying disk so they played ultimate frisbee in the large grassy area behind the main lodge. Even Nicki and Michelle joined in. Michelle was fast and athletic, Jacob thought. Tyler caught a great pass in the end zone. Even though it isn't a contact sport, the entire cabin of Badgers decided to dogpile him. Even the two ladies jumped on him. They all laughed. Children from the other cabin just gawked at them.

All the boys fell asleep seconds after the lights went out that evening. Jacob had another busy and wonderful day. Time was finally starting to go quickly. He would be back in the comforts of his own home playing his video games in no time.

Chapter 9 Tuesday on the Lake

The boys woke up the next morning to Nicki's clapping as she walked down the aisle. "Come on gentlemen, let's get up, it's going to be a nice relaxing day," she said gently. Jacob was just glad that she wasn't pounding on a metal garbage can with a wooden stick like they did in the army movies.

Jacob stretched and made his way to the training schedule. He didn't know why he had to get up if it was going to be a nice relaxing day. It was now, Tuesday, the 18th of June. After breakfast there was a short class on water safety and then the remainder of the day was listed as free time. Nicki announced that after breakfast that they would meet at the lake by the boat house. She said after a short class on water safety they would be free to kayak, paddle board, or swim. She told them to make sure they put on swimming trunks after their morning meal.

The day went by quick as it turned out to be quite enjoyable. Jacob and Tyler often went to their community pool during the summer back home especially if the outside temperature became unbearable. They both were pretty good swimmers. Jacob actually taught Tyler how to swim in just a few days. Nicki still made everyone wear life jackets. Jacob and Tyler had never been on a kayak before. They each had their own kayak and they had fun chasing each other around splashing each other with their oars. Some of the other boys joined in.

After being on the kayak for a bit, Jacob decided he was going to try to use a paddle board. Jacob couldn't get the hang of paddle boarding.

He had trouble standing on it and keeping his balance. Thankfully it was warm that day so he didn't mind getting tossed into the cold lake every time the board flipped him off. Some of the boys swam and others stayed in the shallow end of the lake. There was a dock that extended far into the lake that some of the boys used as a diving board. Nicki kept a watchful eye on the entire cabin of boys.

Jacob sat down to rest near Nicki. She was near the shoreline sitting and basking in the warm mountain sun watching each of her charges play in and around the water. He asked where Michelle was and he was told that she was at the rappelling tower with the other cabin.

Nicki smiled and added, "Jacob, she's a bit old for you. And probably not your type."

Jacob turned red, shook his head, stood up, and walked off. Nicki put her head down and snickered.

After a fast lunch, the boys returned to the lake for a few more hours. Tyler and Jacob swam until they were too tired. They spent the rest of their time on the shoreline hanging out with their camp counselor and watched the other boys play in the warm sun. The boys asked her where she was from.

Nicki was born in Coos Bay on the southern coast of Oregon. She went to the same high school that the famed runner Steve Prefontaine went to. Of course, it was at different times she added. Her eldest uncle went to school with him. Nicki's father was a logger and her mother was a bank teller in town. When she was seven, her father was felling a tree when a large limb broke free and landed on his head killing him instantly. His helmet unfortunately provided no protection that day. Her mother called that limb a widowmaker. Her mother was of course distraught and she vowed to never marry again. Like the two boys, Nicki too was an only child. She ran track in school and played soccer. Growing up, she didn't care for the forest or much of the great outdoors as she always held a resentment for her dad's untimely death. She didn't know who to be angry at; she just wanted to be angry. It gave her a façade of solitude and contentment. As time went by her resentment melted into curiosity as learned that hate and anger were wasted emotions. She decided she wanted to study trees and plants. She was immediately accepted into Oregon State University after graduation and she became a Beaver. During the summer, she spends her time at this Camp.

Before their dinner, they a had few hours in the common room. Josh, Jarod, Tyler, and Jacob all played pool. Josh was actually good at it. He won all of the games. He said his father was a champion billiards player and had taught him everything he knew. Jacob thought that story sounded actually plausible.

That night a few hours before the lights went out, Nicki walked in their cabin. She told them to get a lot of rest. Tomorrow the entire camp was doing a five mile hike out into the woods. They would be having lunch halfway into the hike. Jacob thought to himself that sleeping that evening wouldn't be a problem since he had another busy day at Camp Pertida. The warm sun and water activities had exhausted him. He was looking forward to a good rest; besides a hike, he didn't know what tomorrow would bring.

Chapter 10 Take a Hike

The next morning arrived too fast. It was Wednesday already. Jacob felt like he had just closed his eyes a few moments prior to those awful buzzing lights came on. Nicki, her usual cheerful demeanor, was there ensuring they didn't fall back asleep. This morning she was walking up and down the aisle singing some sort of Army marching song. Michelle probably had taught it to her.

The boys did their usual morning routine. It was almost a ritual now. They showered and cleaned the cabin and the bathroom. Michelle had called it the latrine the other day. They helped each other make their bunks. Nicki reminded them to eat a big healthy breakfast to prepare them for their hike. Then almost like a military platoon they all marched together to grab morning chow.

Jacob snagged some more snacks off the salad bar. He had his tray filled with food. He hadn't had sugar cereal since he was at home. He was really enjoying these banquet-style morning meals. If he ever spoke to his mother again, he might ask for a vegetable stuffed omelet sin mushroom.

The boys returned to their cabin. Nicki was patiently waiting for them at the far end. She had a large hiking backpack on the ground in front of her.

She showed them how to properly pack a rucksack for a day hike. She told them to always pack an extra pair of socks no matter how short a jaunt through the forest might be. They are lightweight and don't take up much room. She told them that wet socks on the feet from sweat or an accidental dip into a stream could end in with sore feet or blisters. She also spoke about something called trench feet. She told them to pack something warm because the weather could change in a heartbeat. Even if the weather called for triple digits, always bring a sweater or coat especially if in the mountains. She gave each child a military looking poncho to put in their bag. She said to take care of them because they were on loan from the camp. They gladly accepted the ponchos. All the kids were well aware that rain was just one of the inconveniences of living in the Pacific Northwest. Oregon was a state where many people carried both sunglasses and rain jackets.

"Hopefully you boys snaked some packaged snacks from the salad bar, if not you will find some extra stuff in your packed lunches," Nicki said.

Each boy walked up and grabbed a sack lunch. She reminded the cabin that dehydration is a killer. Water bottles were filled and checked. They were also given a few water purification tablets as added measure. Only to be used in an emergency she said and then smiled. They would all be back later this afternoon drinking milk and juice.

Some of the boys expressed concerns of walking five miles. The walk to school wasn't even that far and it was mostly flat. Nicki said that a five-mile hike wasn't that bad. Yes, it wasn't going to be a flat hike, but it would be manageable. Most of the camp was going so it would be a nice slow pace. There would also be break along the way to enjoy their lunch. She told the boys to just be mindful of where they stepped and to enjoy the sights. She also told them to try and name as many trees and wild plants along the way. She suggested bringing a paper and pen to write them down. The boys balked at that idea.

Jacob and Tyler filled their backpacks with extra socks and some warm clothing. They also stuffed their newly received poncho in their bag. Their backpacks were now pregnant with unneeded items. They in fact now felt a little heavier than their usual burden they carried to school.

The boys from Cabin B, gear on their backs, moved outside and met up with rest of the campers from Camp Pertida. All the children formed one long single file line. The adult staff situated themselves along the line. Jacob and Tyler stuck to the back. Some of the children that were forced to stay behind due to injury or illness stood outside the lodge with sullen looks upon their faces. One boy had crutches under his arms. Wonder what happened to him, pondered Jacob.

Some other camp counselor was calling out for a girl named Chloe. The girl, smacking on gum, came running out of her cabin with a backpack carelessly slapped around her shoulder. She didn't seem too happy about the impending hike.

"Let's move out," somebody hollered.

Jacob estimated that close to 30 children were on this day hike. Each child wore the camp shirt to show which cabin they belonged to. Jacob and Tyler were the last two children in line with Nicki taking up the very end of the trail.

After a few minutes, the line of children moved. The line moved slowly at first as the front hikers tried to find a comfortable pace. Then the hike sped up and then it slowed down. Jacob thought he was part of one large accordion. After the first mile of walking along, the pace evened out. The children each had a comfortable space between each other and Jacob didn't feel like he was at the tail end of a human squeeze box. The two boys kept quiet each in their own thoughts.

Jacob enjoyed the hike. It was nice to smell the woods and hear the wildlife. Small little squirrels darted in and out of their path. Nicki said one was called a Townsend's chipmunk. They walked next to a stream for several hundred yards. Everything was so green and he enjoyed the sound of the stream as it rushed over rocks and downed trees. Several paths branched from the one path they were on. The column of hikers took the right one. It went away from the creek. The path went up and then down. Overall, they seemed to be climbing up in elevation.

The girl, the one who was late to the hike, was walking in front of Jacob. She seemed to be the same age as Jacob. She had dark long straight hair and green eyes. She almost looked like the younger version of Michelle. Her hair was tied up in back and diamond studded earrings glistened in the daylight. She kept looking back at him. Jacob thought she was sort of cute. His fondness for girls, he thought to himself, had just appeared out of nowhere recently.

She finally spoke to Jacob, "where are you from? You look familiar."

"Well, I have been at this camp since Saturday."

"No," she replied, "before this I mean, where are you from, Portland? I haven't seen you on Snapchat or TikTok, have I?"

"No, I am from the Salem area. I am not really into social media."

"Oh," she said sounding disappointed.

About that time someone was yelling for Nicki.

"Hey, Nicki, we need you up here real quick," an adult yelled out from somewhere up front. It sounded urgent. Kids turned their head back and repeated the same message down towards the rear of the line.

Jacob turned his head and was about ready to repeat it, but Nicki put up her hand, smiled, and nodded, "I heard, I heard."

Nicki told Tyler and Jacob to keep up with the rest of the kids. She said she would be right back. She cinched up her backpack across her chest and ran up the column of marching kids. In a matter of seconds, she disappeared beyond the long column of walking campers.

The two hikers continued their march forward keeping the other kids in front in their view. They seemed to be moving faster so Jacob told the girl in front of him to hurry her pace. She seemed like she had better places to be. He was afraid that they would lose the rest of the hikers. The girl turned her head towards Jacob intent on saying something rude when she tripped over a giant rock that jutted out in their hiking path. She sprawled forward instinctively placing her hands out in front of her as she slammed down on a fallen log. She cried out. Both boys ran up to her.

"Are you okay?" Tyler asked.

She was crying. She had a cut above her left eye that was beginning to bleed. Her arms were skinned up. Tyler repeated his question.

Through sobs she said she thought she was hurt. She was blaming Jacob for making her fall. The boys helped her up. She dusted herself off. The boys tried to get her to walk. She limped favoring her left leg. She winced trying to move forward. Besides her bleeding cut, she had scrapes and scratches on her face. That downed piece of timber had not been kind to her.

"I think I need to sit down for a second," she said glaring at Jacob. Jacob felt bad and decided it would be a good idea not to respond. He hoped she didn't suffer a concussion.

The girl sat on the very log that had arrested her fall and caused the unfortunate condition she now found herself in. She checked herself over, looking at her skinned-up elbows and hands.

Jacob knelt next to her. He and Tyler were concerned that she could be badly injured. Tyler took out a clean white handkerchief out of his pocket and pressed it to the cut above her eye. Jacob questioned to himself what Tyler was doing with a handkerchief. Who carries handkerchiefs around these days besides old men and well-meaning aunts?

Jacob then looked up towards the trail. He was going to call out to stop the hike. There was nobody in sight. A tingle ran up his nose. Jacob got that sharp tingle every time something traumatic was about to happen. That tingle reminded him of chlorinated water that ran up his nose when he went upside down in a swimming pool. It was like he was on that tower all over again. He got that tinge when he almost fell out of a tree when he was nine. Although he was close the other day, he had never had a panic attack, but if he was to have one, now would be an appropriate time.

He yelled out frantically, "hey guys wait for us!"

No answer. It was quiet as if the entire forest suddenly vacated at once. Not a sound. The ground squirrels were gone. Even the birds must have sensed something and they too decided to depart the area in search of more familiar trees.

He screamed again cupping his mouth with his hands. Tyler was busy looking over the hurt girl.

Jacob didn't know what to do. He couldn't leave the girl there. He ran about 30 yards forward and saw that the path they were on split into two hiking trails; one going down to the creek again and another heading up another long hill. Fresh footprints of all sizes went in both directions. He turned around to get back to Tyler and the girl. He called out again this time with all of his might.

No answer.

Out of breath, Jacob sputtered, "I don't know which way the group went."

Tyler spoke up, "we should just head back to camp, there is no use trying to find the main group."

The girl agreed, "let's head back, I think I can walk." Looking at Jacob she sneered, "this is your fault, kid."

The three kids turned around and walked along the trail. The sun was now directly above them. The girl limped along. The two boys slowed down so she could keep up. From out of nowhere they heard rustling beyond the trees. Jacob's heart sank, he was thinking it was a cougar or a bear. Whatever it was, it was coming their way from deep within the tree line. The forest was thick with tall trees and brush. He couldn't see very far into the tree line. The noise stopped. Jacob, thought, great we are being stalked by some wild animal. Jacob only a few minutes earlier was enjoying the outdoors, now he loathed it. How things can change so quickly.

The sound came again. It was getting louder. Limbs were snapping, the ground was being trampled. The kids froze.

Then from out of nowhere, Ryden jumped out of the tree line. He screamed waving his arms in the air. The three kids stood there too stricken to move. The girl yelped in terror.

"Got you guys," laughed Ryden, "you should 'ave seen your dumb faces."

Chapter 11 Forming the Band

Nicki was upset to find out that there was no real emergency. Someone had a question about a dead animal they had just stumbled across. It was pretty fresh. The carrions hadn't even got to it yet. It turned out to be a very dead hoary marmot. She wondered in irritation why the other adult camp counselors couldn't have pointed that out. The line of hikers had stretched out pretty far. Thankfully there were experienced adults scattered along the way that knew the route in case the kids got too separated from each other.

She decided to make her way back to the end of the hiking line. Passing the children, she thought it would be a good idea to get a headcount. She was positive that it never occurred to the other adults to count the children. They left camp with 33 kiddos. She counted each child, 29. She got to Zach and Josh who were one of the last children at the end of the column of hikers. She ran up the line and then back down again. Same number, 29. She asked the adults if they had lost anyone. They thought that everyone was accounted for.

Speaking to Josh and Zach, she asked, "Where's Tyler, Jacob, and the girl?" She now began questioning herself on who the fourth camper might be.

Josh turned his head towards the rear. He shrugged his shoulders, "I thought they were behind us."

Nicki called out front to another camp counselor who was up the line of kids, "Hey Joe, JOE! Hey, we are missing four kids." Looking at

Josh and Zach, she said, "I told Jacob to stay up with you guys." Josh shrugged his shoulders. Zach pushed his glasses up to his face.

Joe, a heavyset camp counselor, face red as a beet, and out of breath, came waddling towards Nicki. He had one hand wrapped around the waistband of his cargo shorts lest they fall down as he lumbered towards the blonde camp counselor.

Nicki had a lump in her throat. This was her second year as a counselor and prior to this event never lost a camper. "We need to check the children, see who else is missing."

Joe stood there with a blank look on his red face. Beads of sweat had formed on his face. He was bent down, his hands now on his knees.

"Who's missing?" Nicki called out, she repeated louder, "who is missing?"

About then, a boy from Cabin A came up and said, "I think it's Ryden, I thought he was behind me. He was throwing rocks at me earlier."

Another boy came up and added, "Yeah it's Ryden. He was walking in front of me, looked up and he was gone."

"Joe, I need you stay in the rear; I need to go find my kids."

Joe, trying to catch his breath, asked, "do you need me to have everyone stop? I am more than happy to have the kids wait here."

"Just keep going, stop at the designated place for lunch. We will catch up," answered Nicki.

Joe was obviously disappointed with that response and so he called out to have the kids to continue moving.

Nicki sprinted down the path from where the campers had come from.

Jacob who had been frightened to death was now seething with anger. His hate for this kid just deepened. He was already scared that they lost sight of their fellow hikers and now this turd came out of nowhere to scare them senseless.

"Where did you come from?" Snapped Jacob. It was difficult to hide his anger.

"Had to go pee, came back and saw the group had left. Heard you through the trees. So, I figured I would scare you idiots."

"I don't know what you plan on doing and really don't care, but she's hurt, and we are heading back to camp," Jacob said with a frustrated tone.

Tyler, Jacob, and the injured girl continued their walk down the path. Jacob took the girl's rucksack. Ryden stood there. He didn't say anything. After a long pause, he decided to follow the other three.

They came to a fork in the path and stopped. Jacob was certain that if they took the one on the right it would lead them back to the creek; the one they were next to earlier. He stood there second guessing himself. Frankly, he hadn't really paid attention to where they were going when he was with the rest of the group. He was busy taking in the sights. He really never had been in the wild before coming to Camp Pertida.

"Well, which way, smart boy?" Asked the bully.

Jacob really didn't know. He looked at Tyler and then at the girl. They both slowly shook their heads.

"Listen," the girl now changed her mind, "I heard if you get lost you should stay put. Maybe we should stay here. We were on this very trail with the rest of the kids, the group or some camp counselor will probably be along shortly."

Tyler pointed out that her cut above her eye was still bleeding. It didn't look like it was ready to stop. It was probably best to get back to the lodge so the camp nurse could get a look at it. It probably needed stitches and some antiseptic. He didn't think they were too far away.

Ryden spoke up and pointing left said, "I think it's this way you morons."

Jacob had about enough of Ryden. He had never been in a fight and this kid would probably pound him into the dirt. He wanted to punch him so badly. Jacob jaw was clenched. He wanted to tell him that he didn't really care what he thought. Instead, Jacob remained silent. His brain was going way too fast to make any decisions. He just knew that Ryden's presence only added to the extreme stress of the situation.

Ryden without waiting for an answer moved forward down the path he had pointed at. The others decided to follow despite Jacob's gut telling him otherwise.

The kids walked for several minutes, maybe close to 30. Jacob didn't know. He came to a stop. None of this looked familiar or maybe it did. He didn't know. Everything now all looked the same. Each tree looked exactly like the other tree. Each tree was a clone of the other Jacob thought. The path looked exactly like the path they were on earlier. But then again maybe the hiking trail from earlier wasn't exactly like this one. He asked himself, what would Forced Renegade do? Nothing, because Forced Renegade is fake, made-up nonsense, played by some British dude that had never once picked up a real comic book.

"Can we rest for a second?" Asked the girl. Her cut above her eye was bleeding again. She was able to stop it for a bit. She looked exhausted.

The kids sat down except for Ryden.

The girl pulled out a cell phone. It was bedazzled with glitter and pink sequin. She raised it and then moved it left and then to the right. She was trying to catch a signal.

Ryden sneered, "uh, you are not supposed to have that. Having trouble updating your Instagram?"

The girl glared at him and mocked, "uh, looks like I do have it, fatty. My mom uses Instagram thank you. I use TikTok."

Tyler wanted to change the subject and asked her name.

"It's Chloe," she said rolling her eyes.

Ryden looked at her up and down, "well that name's fitting with your expensive phone, diamond earrings, and designer jeans. Surprised that backpack isn't made by Lewis Boo-ton. Bet you're from, let me guess...Goose Hollow, the Pearl District, somewhere in the West Hills."

Jacob didn't recognize the neighborhood names. Tyler bent to his side and whispered in Jacob's ear, "rich neighborhoods in Portland." He wanted to know, briefly, if she happened to live anywhere near his father.

Chloe snapped back, "it's pronounced Louis Vuitton, you overweight moron. Not that it's any of your business, I am from Lake Oswego. And let me guess, wait, don't tell me, you've recently escaped from the MacLaren Youth Correctional Facility or perhaps fat camp."

Tyler was ready to bend to his side and whisper in his buddy's ear again. Jacob stopped him and whispered, "I know Tye, juvenile detention for boys in Woodburn."

Ryden gave out an obnoxious laugh, "figures that you're from Lake Oswego, not that surprised. How are you surviving without internet access? This is probably your first exposure to the outside world. Let me introduce you to the forest, I am sure you read about it on your app."

Chloe couldn't be bothered to respond to the boy's banal comments. She just pressed her hand against her head with one hand and rubbed her leg with the other.

Tyler pulled out his sack lunch. He fished out a double decker peanut butter sandwich. He took a large bite out of it. He then eagerly swallowed the rest of it down. He pulled out his canteen and swigged a bit of water to loosen up the peanut butter that felt lodged in his throat. He then opened up a bag of barbecue flavored potato chips.

Jacob was sick to his stomach. It was in a knot. He didn't think he could eat. How could his best friend eat at a time like this? He sat looking at the tall green trees, wild grass, and ferns that seemed to be everywhere. He knew they were now officially lost. His mind went into several directions. His thoughts were scattered like dead leaves after a heavy storm. Do they stay put; do they move? Will they be found by Nicki and the rest? Will they ever find Camp Pertida? Do the others even realize that they are missing? When will the adults find out that they are missing four campers, when they do a headcount before lights out? He then thought about his mom and how this was somehow her fault. If it wasn't for her, he would be safely tucked away in his bedroom playing a video game.

After some thought, Jacob stood up, "it's time to get moving, guys. We can't stay here. Chloe needs help."

Chloe said her leg felt better but the cut above her eye wouldn't stop bleeding. She was pressing Tyler's blood-soaked handkerchief against her forehead. Despite the wound, she was ready to move.

Chloe said, "these hiking trails must all lead to something, if we stick on one, it should lead us to safety, right?"

Ryden spoke up, "do you even have thoughts of your own? Changing your mind again? So, who left you in charge, you rich bi-"

Tyler finally had enough, he had been very quiet up to this point. He jumped into Ryden's face and gave him a shove before he could get the word out. Ryden was caught off guard and stumbled backwards a few feet. Angered, he charged back at Tyler. He was now standing directly in front of Tyler. Tyler's face was in the bully's chest. Ryden's fist were clinched and he was ready to strike.

"Jump up and push me again you little chump. Oh, sorry, you ARE standing, ghetto boy. I will floor you. Trying to protect this rich girl." Ryden was red in the face and he was livid. He then looked over to Chloe, "I don't think daddy would approve of his precious princess dating a little..." Ryden paused and with disgust was now looking at Tyler up and down. He was thinking hard about using that derogatory term.

"Say it, say it," Tyler said in a low growl with his fist clinched. He was shaking and his face was contorted in a scowl. "I dare you to say it! I want you to say it."

Jacob had never once seen Tyler so riled up, so angry. Yeah, their little town had its flaws, but open racism wasn't one of them. Jacob was sure ignorant people from his small little town said stupid things about poor people, the migrants that worked the neighboring fields, and other minorities like his buddy Tyler. They just never said it to Tyler's face, not that Jacob was aware of. Tyler never told Jacob if kids said anything racist to him at school. Todd Foster was petulant because he enjoyed looking down on people who were poor and those that didn't play sports as well as him. Even Todd never uttered a racist word, well, at least not in front of Jacob.

Ryden had a wicked smile upon his evil face and the word was forming in his mouth ready to get spat out with naked depravity. As the beginning of that awful word started to come out of his mouth, Tyler's right fist came flying like a jackhammer to Ryden's nose, like it was shot out of a canon. The crunch of the cartilage was unmistakable. Blood immediately sprayed out. The large kid fell as if an unknown force had paralyzed his legs from beneath his body. He didn't fall forward or backwards, he just dropped straight down. He was quiet for several moments.

"You broke my nose, you broke my nose, I was only kidding," cried Ryden now in a fetal position; his hands were covering his injured nose. Tears were streaming from his eyes and warm blood seeped through his cupped hands.

Jacob knelt next to him and he wanted to tell him so badly that he got knocked out. He would have added in colorful language he had learned for good measure. He saw that in a movie once. Probably a movie his mother wouldn't have approved of. He wanted to kneel next to him and laugh. He was incredibly proud of his friend that had so galanty stood up for himself and a girl he didn’t even know.

Chloe bit her lip to keep from laughing. There was a small smile beginning to sprout on her scratched up face.

Jacob was still kneeling next to the injured boy. "Probably shouldn't judge a book by its cover," Jacob observed morosely. Despite all the things he wanted to say to Ryden he thought he would be the better person. Tyler actions were the loudest.

Jacob looked at his friend's hands. It was busted up a little. Tyler was shaking it and then opening and closing it. He was trying to get feeling back into it. He was still trembling.

The little ruckus Jacob observed had only got his mind off momentarily of the terrible misfortune they had found themselves in. He was back to worrying about their plight. Ryden was still writhing on the ground like a wounded animal. Blood had darkened the forest ground. He was moaning. Tyler was eyeing his right hand and Chloe, suffering from her own injuries, was staring at the hurt kid on the ground with a sense of wicked curiosity.

Jacob more talking to himself said, "great, three quarters of our little quartet are injured. Guess what, we are still lost folks."

The sun was beginning to set behind the tall evergreen landscape. Its light scattered about the heavily forested floor. Jacob had just noticed that their trail they had been on had narrowed. It was no longer very wide and it wasn't beaten down by years of laden boots like the other trails they had been on.

Tyler spoke up, "listen, we were heading southeast on 26 with your mom, right? Maybe more south than east?

Jacob answered, "yeah, it's what it showed on her GPS."

"So, we made a right off the highway and traveled several miles to camp, so then we were traveling more west, right?"

"Look Tye, I love that you are talking so much, maybe punching that kid turned on your jabbering switch, but tell me where you are going with this." Jacob was boring into his friend's eyes. Jacob was highly irritated at this point. He had always been haunted by anxiety, but this was on an entirely different level.

"We went deeper into the woods on our hike and didn't cross a major road. I am thinking if we head east or at least northeast we should run back onto highway 26 if not some other forest road. Heck, we might even walk right into the camp. We drove by countless forest roads on the highway last Saturday before turning onto Pertida Road. The sun is starting to set west so if we keep it on our backs we should find a road, hopefully the highway or another road."

Ryden was trying to get on his feet, he looked like a draft horse trying to get on its feet after a short nap. His nose was still bleeding profusely. Both of his eyes were beginning to turn a dark purple. He couldn't manage to get up so Tyler walked over and extended his hand. Ryden, with his left hand clamped on his injured nose and his head tilted up, reluctantly took Tyler's hand.

After Ryden steadied himself, with a tinge of defeat and extremely nasally, he said, "Mike Tyson is right, we should do what he says."

Chloe agreed. Her bleeding on her forehead had temporarily stopped. It was quite the gash but the blood had coagulated enough that it was no longer bleeding profusely into her left eye. She pulled out her phone again and said that there was still no signal.

Chapter 12 Wednesday Noonish

Nicki had run all the way back to camp. She took the exact same hiking path that all the kids and adults had taken. She yelled into the forest the entire way without luck. She scrambled into each cabin frantically looking for the boys and girl. She looked behind the cabins to see if the children were there.

She hurried into the main lodge turned a corner and ran literally into the camp administrator, Ms. Betty Holstrom. Nicki had almost knocked her down. Ms. Holstrom was a short thin lady, with straight black hair, that dressed like she was still stuck in 1978. She always wore the same flowery skirt, puke green blouse, and cheap Velcro tennis shoes. She also had pearls around her skinny neck. No matter the outside weather, she always had an oversized button up yellow Afghan sweater. It hung on her like an oversized canopy. Cat hair clung on her oversized sweater for dear life. Her tethered red cat-eye spectacles rested on her long thin bird nose. She was middle aged and never found the time to marry. She smelled of old lady perfume like sweet vanilla with a hint of expired baby powder.

"Miss Vanderworker, can I help you?" Huffed Ms. Holstrom. She never addressed adults by their first name. She didn't like to get too personal with any of her employees. She probably called her own parents by their last name. Nicki had a love hate relationship with her own last name. Maybe it was the way Ms. Holstrom said it, laced with an acidic and irritable pronunciation.

"I am looking for four lost children. Lost 'em on the hike," she then rattled off the names, "Jacob Hart, Tyler Jackson, Ryden Nielsen, and Chloe Farmington." Nicki was out of breath. Even though she had always been athletic, she never remembered running so quickly.

"How did you ever manage to lose four children on a five-mile hike, Miss Vanderworker?" The word "you" was highly accentuated as if she was the only adult that bothered to show up to the hike that day.

Nicki avoided the question and said, "look, we need to start a search party, call the sheriff, you know, search and rescue, some sort of authority."

Ms. Holstrom guffawed and rolled her eyes, "you think I am going to call in the cavalry? May I remind you that this is a place of business! I don't need parents up in arms. The owners of this place will lose their minds. Parents pay a pretty penny to have their children safely housed here during the summer. Big business pays us a fortune to have their events out here. For Pete's sake, the Knights had a wedding here last fall! We are the premiere camp of the Pacific Northwest. No missy, absolutely NOT. You are going to get the rest of the kids back here and you will organize a search party with the adult staff. We will have them found and back before dinner! Why are you still standing here? GO!"

"I always wondered where you got your benevolent and warm personality," answered Nicki, of course the sarcasm was said only in her head. Instead, without saying a word, she turned around to get back on the trail so she could adhere to her malevolent supervisor's orders.

That afternoon, while Nicki was in full on panic mode, Jennifer went to the office that belonged to Bright Beacon Investigation. The conversation she had with the stranger on Saturday was still nagging at her. The business was housed in an old beautiful blue cottage with a stepped porch that sat next to the 100-acre Bush Park in Salem. It's a beautiful wooded park that has a Victorian house on it that was built on the north side around 1878. The beautiful historic house had been turned into a museum by the city. A lot of those old homes that were built on the west side of the park in the historic district had been turned into businesses. Jennifer went into the old converted house and was met by a male receptionist.

"Can I help you, ma'am?" Asked the assistant. He was a young pleasant looking man with a trimmed beard and pointed nose. He had a flowery teacup in his hand.

"I am looking for a Mr. Paul," answered Jennifer.

"Yes, do you have an appointment?" He kindly asked.

"Um, no, just a question."

About this time, a short stocky middle-aged man with muscles that stretched his short sleeved collared polo shirt came walking out of one of the rooms. He had a faded tattoo of an anchor on his right forearm. He had short gray hair that sat on the perimeter of his balding head. His gray eyes and smile showed that he had a friendly disposition. He must have overheard the conversation.

"I'm Bill Paul, who might you be?" He said warmly. He had his hand extended. He had a big grin. A large space between his two front teeth made him even more genial.

Jennifer extended her hand and shook his with a lot of hesitation, "Jennifer, Jennifer Hart, but you are not Bill Paul."

The man had a jovial laugh and said, "I can promise you, ma'am that is my name."

Jennifer looked very confused. She told the investigator about the man that had showed up on her doorstep on the previous Saturday claiming he was Bill Paul from BBI. She told him that the man sounded very convincing and even had a business card. He was so convincing she told him where her son was at.

The man standing in front of her pulled out a card of his own from his wallet along with his driver's license.

"Like this one?" Asked the investigator handing over his business card.

"Yes, exactly like this one," said Jennifer in a deflated tone.

"Hmmm...Was he a tall man, I mean very tall, by any chance, lot of muscles? Hard to understand English accent?"

"He was extremely tall and muscular, brown hair and eyes. Looked a little menacing. Maybe mid 30s. Had a man waiting in the car. No accent, wait, he said 'cheers, love' when he left."

"Had two men in here last week, one didn't say much, very stout, seemed grumpy. The tall one did all the talking said he was looking to hire an investigator to help find his wife who fled the United Kingdom. Supposedly, according to him, she moved to South Salem. They did seem a bit sketchy. He didn't go into too much detail, but took a couple of my cards, said he would be in touch."

Jennifer's heart almost stopped. The coloring left her face. She didn't know to be angered or to be worried. She was upset with herself for being duped by that stranger.

"I noticed you don't have a cell number on your card." Jennifer commented.

"Yeah, I don't need every person having my cell number. They can call my office and I'm pretty good at getting back to them. I still use a flip phone you see." He took out an old flip phone from a leather holster attached to his belt. "And I would rather not have it, does come in handy I suppose."

He could see that Jennifer seemed distressed. He tried to comfort her. "Look, perhaps you should call the police and call that camp your son went to. I am not sure what those guys are up to. They seemed a little wishy-washy the more I think about their visit. Call me if you need anything, or at least my office. If those guys took my card for nefarious reasons, the least I can do is help you out."

Jennifer left the little cottage and got into her car. She immediately called Camp Pertida. It rang and rang. Finally, after several rings, a voice with exasperation answered. It was Ms. Holstrom. Jennifer didn't go into her encounter with the man on Saturday or the conversation she just had with the real Mr. Paul. Instead, she just wanted to hear her son's voice. Ms. Holstrom assured Jennifer that her son was safe. He was out on a hike with the rest of the children enjoying his time in the mountains. She would have his camp counselor Ms. Nicki Vanderworker contact her later that evening. Then the snippety lady hung up on Jennifer without as so much as a goodbye.

Jacob's mother then called the Salem Police Department. They didn't seem very helpful nor did they seem very interested in Jennifer's concerns. There wasn't anything the police could do without a crime. They suggested if she was worried about her son, she should just drive up to Camp Pertida and pull him out.

She reluctantly returned home. She would wait for Nicki to call. Perhaps she was overthinking the whole thing. This could all be just a big misunderstanding. Hopefully.

Chapter 13 What is a Game Trail?

The four children in fact all agreed to head east and walked away from the setting sun. They left the trail that was about to make a dogleg back westerly. They tramped on the forest floor and found a smaller trail that was heading in their direction. They were very determined to find a road or the camp.

"This is a small trail," observed Chloe.

Ryden who was still nursing his nose was now a bit more tolerable. He said, "It's a game trail."

"Game trail?" Asked the girl.

"Yeah, my uncle takes me hunting in the fall, it's a trail that has been formed by bigger animals, like deer or elk. Not really made by hikers. My uncle says that animals will take the path of least resistance to conserve their energy," explained Ryden.

Tyler had taken point and was walking with a sense of confidence. He turned his head around every so often to ensure his companions were still behind him. Jacob was still reeling from being lost and had kept quiet. He was upset at himself for being so scared. He pondered on what his friend thought of him now. It didn't seem like Tyler was his sidekick any longer, his little buddy.

They had walked for what seemed like forever. They had no idea how long they had been walking. The forest seemed like it wouldn't end. They must have been in a depression because they couldn't see any outstanding terrain features like other hills or mountains. They were small little creatures treading on forest duff overshadowed and dwarfed by 100 plus foot trees. The sun was beginning to set behind them. Tyler had asked Chloe if she could pull out her phone to see if there was signal. She fished out her phone only to inform them that it had died. The battery had died on her phone while it continued to search in vain for a cell tower.

The forest opened up a bit. The children were now in a small grassy meadow. They scared a large doe and her fawn who were munching on feed on the far side of the grassland. The deer quickly jumped away darting back into the tree stand as quiet as mice. Jacob didn't realize that deer could hop so high.

Seeing that the sun was dipping well below the canopy of the tree line, Tyler told the group that it was probably time to set up camp. He estimated that it was probably after eight in the evening. It would be just about an hour or so before the sun dissolved behind the western trees stealing the light and heat of the summer day. They were all very disappointed that they yet had found a road.

Tyler found a bare spot in the meadow and found rocks to make a large fire ring. He instructed Jacob and Ryden to go and find downed wood. He told Chloe to rest her leg. The two boys had quite the haul and brought back plenty of wood. There had been a major fire in the area they were in several years back and there was still burnt and dead timber that laid all around.

Tyler untied his tennis shoe pulling the string out. He used his shoestring to fashion a bow drill with a curved stick that one of the other boys had found. He found a small sharp rock and began to use it to sand another stick. The third stick was much bigger and a bit flatter, more like a limb. Ryden, with a mischievous smile on his battered face, handed Tyler a pocket knife. Tyler was thankful he hadn't been stabbed by it earlier. He used it to cut away wood making a depression in the flatter limb. Jacob brought over small bits of wood, small strips of bark, and other forest detritus and duff. They made a small woody ball out of it. Before they knew it, smoke was beginning to billow out of the small pile of wood debris. Tyler was lightly blowing on it. In just a few seconds, much to their surprise, the wood caught on fire. Jacob was impressed. He marveled in amazement; was this the same quiet and reserved Tyler that he went to school with?

Tyler suggested that they all remove their socks and dry them near the fire. Each one pulled off their shoes and peeled off their dirty socks. Jacob curled his toes. It felt nice to have shoes off his feet. He had no idea how many miles they had walked that first day. It was definitely more than five.

The sun in fact took the warmth with it as it dipped below the horizon. The heat from the blazing fire was nice. The kids gathered around sitting down barefooted. The forest was quiet apart from the crackling fire and the children were reticent. There was something primitive and soothing about a campfire that brought a sense of solace to their dire situation.

Jacob felt hungry, but his stomach was still in knots. He had told himself that he wanted to go camping but this wasn't what he had in mind. The fire brought a little peace to his overactive mind but it didn't stir up any hunger.

Tyler was poking a large stick in the fire. He was deep in thought. After several moments of silence, he looked up at Ryden, "I am sorry, man, I shouldn't have thrown hands. I lost my temper."

Ryden looked up, his nose had stopped bleeding a while ago. "I deserved it. I can be a jerk. It was an epic punch though. I figured I heard that word enough times at home, it was okay to say. My dad can say some awful things."

Jacob asked Ryden where he was from. He wanted to break up the awkwardness that was in the air. Jacob still wasn't sure of him.

"Gresham," answered Ryden.

It was quiet again. Tyler was still moving hot coals around with his stick. The reflection from the flames shimmered on his thoughtful face. "My mother was originally from Gresham."

Jacob was surprised to hear Tyler talk about his mother again. First at the comic convention and now sitting around a campfire.

"She met my dad after he moved from the south. He's from Tennessee. He still roots for Vanderbilt. He came to Oregon to look for work. Always worked on big trucks, my dad, I mean."

Tyler said no more. Jacob wanted to press him so badly. He wanted to find out more about his friend and his mom. He didn't know what to say. Jacob remained silent looking at the dark landscape beyond their fire.

Ryden spoke up. "Both my parents are from Gresham, as far as I know. My father doesn't tell me much, he's too busy drinking. My mother left both of us about two years ago. She went to go get cigarettes and never returned. When he's drinking, he's beating me, and when he's sober, he's beating me. Blames me for my mom walking out." He paused and pointed to the scar above his eye. "That's when he got upset that I walked in front of him when he was watching the World Series. The only alone time I have is when he is at work; he's an electrician. Thankfully he works long hours. Sometimes my uncle takes me, surprised those two are even related."

Chloe finally spoke up, "I am sorry, Ryden."

Ryden said, "nothing to be sorry about."

Jacob turned to Chloe, "what's your story?" He was trying to make his apology for her fall. Maybe it was his fault that they were in this mess. He shouldn't have tried talking to her when they were hiking with the rest of the campers. If she hadn't turned her head and tumbled, they would be back at the camp playing table tennis or listening to one of Josh's outlandish stories.

"I'm from Lake Oswego," she laughed. "Which you guys know. Thankfully no brothers or sisters. My parents haven't left me, but they might as well have. They both own this large knife company in Stumptown. I see them for a few moments in the morning. They practically grunt their goodbyes to me, like I am some sort of burden. They probably wouldn't care if they knew I was missing." She chucked a rock as far as she could as if to emphasize her dissatisfaction with her family.

Jacob didn't say anything but understood what it was like to have absent parents. Maybe all these kids weren't so different from one another.

Chloe asked out loud if they would be eaten by any large animals that night. Ryden said that they should be safe if they stayed together and kept the fire going throughout the night. He said it was probably not a good idea to be walking just before sunset or at dawn; he heard that's when the cougars like to hunt.

Tyler added more wood to the warm fire and it crackled and lit up brighter. Tyler took out his poncho and wrapped up in it. The three other kids followed suit. The borrowed ponchos actually proved to be quite thick and warm. They used their backpacks as pillows.

Jacob, his anxiety near its threshold, couldn't sleep. His stress was in full gear. He couldn't get comfortable. His camping companions were fast asleep. Tyler was slightly snoring. Ryden was outright loudly sleeping with a guttural sound of an irate zombie. He sounded like an overweight old man, Jacob thought. His broken schnoz probably didn't help. Chloe was the only quiet one. Her breathing was barely audible. Jacob thought she looked like an angel, despite her ugly gash above her eye and her scratched up face. Jacob turned again and finally out of exasperation sat up and tossed another piece of wood in the fire. He thought he heard movement beyond the meadow. A few branches snapped in the distance.

Jacob waited. He wasn't ready to wake up the others. More movement and then it was followed by silence. Many minutes passed without any other noise. Jacob decided to lie down again. He listened intently and thought he heard another noise in the distance. Nothing. He still couldn't sleep. How could they sleep at a time like this? He tried to calm down his breathing. He counted his breaths. There were no clouds in the sky. The stars were bright. He could see the Big Dipper. There was a bright yellow star that stood out in the eastern sky. He was curious to know if it was Mars. He followed a low orbiting satellite that silently swept across the night sky. Every time he got cold, he tossed another piece of wood in the fire. After several hours he eventually dozed off.

Nicki and most of the adult counselor searched for the lost kids until the sun retired that Wednesday. They searched every nearby trail. They retraced their hiking trail steps from earlier. The other campers had to stay in the lodge's dayroom under the scornful eye of Ms. Holstrom.

The search party came back empty handed and breaking the news to Ms. Holstrom was not easy. To say she was livid would have been a gross understatement. She gathered her staff together into the cafeteria.

She looked like a bespectacled vulture with her oversized sweater rising up around her long-bent neck. She yanked off her red glasses, they now swung on the chain lanyard around her thin neck. Glaring at each one of the counselors she seethed, "listen you mindless dimwits, you will resume your search at daybreak. Go in pairs. This will not get out, do you understand? Not a word of this will get out. I will need two counselors to stay back and entertain the kids. Cancel tomorrow's activities, they can all stay in the common room or the gym. Turn on the television for them, I don't care. If this gets out to the public, to the parents, to the authorities, I will fire every damn one of you. Guaranteed. You will be lucky to find a career at a second-hand thrift store." She promptly stormed out leaving the others with their mouths gaped.

Nicki quietly left the cafeteria. She couldn't bear to speak with the other staff members. She was close to tears as she entered the hallway.

Ms. Holstrom grabbed Nicki's arm with her boney fingers. With a low sullen voice, she said "you need to call Jennifer Hart. She is worried about her son. Call her back and tell her he is fine, just went to bed. We had a long day. He had a nice uneventful hike in the woods today. He will try and call back tomorrow. In fact, let's make the call together, shall we?"

Nicki made the call to Jennifer. Ms. Holstrom stood so close to her that she could feel her hot breath and smell her awful perfume. Jennifer told her about her conversation with the real investigator in Salem. Nicki assured her not to worry and told her she would have her son call as soon as possible. Nicki was so guilt stricken that she puked in the staff bathrooms.

Chapter 14 Thursday with a View

The children woke up to a cold light drizzle early the next morning. Despite the overhead clouds, the sun was just making its way up on the eastern horizon spilling morning light through the trees that stood beyond the meadow. The children could see their breath. Their fire was cold, only a single string of smoke slowly rose from a blackened piece of wood.

The kids gathered their belongings. They each kicked dirt over the dead fire. It was a cold summer morning. They didn't bother speaking to each other. They had their ponchos draped over their bodies. They looked like camouflaged ghosts. The band of four marched toward the rising sun.

Nicki woke up to rain like the lost children. She had probably slept three hours. She quickly got dressed and headed outside. She saw Michelle pulling into the staff parking in her '97 blue Toyota 4runner. She had the previous day off so she stayed at a historic lodge in Zig Zag. Nicki quickly told her of the previous day's events. She suggested to Michelle that since she had military experience maybe she should lead the search party among the staff members.

Michelle gathered the adults together in the employee lounge. Much to his own relief, Joe was one of the two camp counselors asked to stay behind and watch the remaining kids. There were ten adults available to search, a few of them were from the office. This was all that

Ms. Holstrom could muster? Nicki was disgusted. One of the staffers had high heels on!

Michelle had found a large map of the Mt. Hood Forest area. She had already been to the supply office and gathered several items for her brief. She haphazardly taped the map against the wall. She had been on this trail many times before and the camp always used the same route for the five-mile hike. Using a laser, she pointed to where the camp was located. She used a highlighter to indicate the hiking trail that was taken yesterday. She also highlighted the Cedar Swamp Creek that the trail paralleled. She showed possible routes the kids could have taken to try to get to a road or back to camp. She said most likely they would have stayed on wide hiking paths and hopefully they would stay out of the thick forest. She broke the adult staff into five groups and gave each pair a whistle, a handheld radio, a map, and a compass. Using the map, she assigned each group a specific area to search. She reminded them to look for smoke from a fire or any recent litter. They would meet back at the trailhead at noon sharp.

"Take snacks and plenty of water, it could be a long day," admonished Michelle as she released the searchers to their task.

Michelle and Nicki left for the area they were assigned. Michelle put her arm around Nicki and told her that everything would be okay. Michelle wasn't sure how well the other staff would do on their searching endeavor.

Thankfully the morning rain dissipated for the lost hikers. The clouds had melted away and the sky turned to a beautiful blue. It was beginning to warm up. The children climbed up a rather large hill. It was an old growth area occupied by both firs and red cedar. The diameter of the trees looked big enough to completely block a two-lane highway. Some of the massive trees they were surrounded by had been seedlings when folks still traveled by horse and carriage. The hill kept going up and up. The angle seemed to increase as they treaded along. All four had slipped on the loose ground as they made their ascent. The children were trying to catch their breath as the elevation got higher. They lost the sun as they clambered up the hill, however, Tyler was certain they were heading in the correct direction.

They finally summited the treacherous hill. It had opened up with a thinned-out tree stand on top. There were several stumps and a few fallen trees. They were out of breath. Chloe had her hands on her knees panting. She had been favoring her leg again. Ryden plopped on the ground and then he lay back on his back.

Tyler rose up and pointed, "that's Mount Hood."

Sure enough, in the distance, almost northwest of their present location, stood the stratovolcano, Mount Hood. It sat elegantly with snow still covering its broad shoulders and its pinnacle. Jacob thought the mountain was the nicest looking thing he had seen in quite some time. It looked close enough to touch. It was a surreal feeling to be on top of a large hill looking over a vast amount of forest that stood below them. It looked like miles upon miles of forest land.

They all gave each other congratulatory high fives and then they all simply sat down on a large fir that had fell victim to a strong windstorm that swept over the hilltop sometime in the past. They were exhausted and famished. They each pulled out snacks. They still had part of their lunch. In fact, Jacob didn't eat any of his lunch from the previous day. Jacob had new hope now and his stomach wasn't tied up in knots, well, not as badly. He engulfed his peanut butter sandwich with a hunger he had never felt. It was the best sandwich he had ever eaten. Tyler handed Ryden a Vienna sausage. After they ate, they rested for about an hour regaining their strength.

With renewed excitement, they went down the other side of the hill. The sun was quickly moving across the blue sky, but they maintained their heading. As they went down the hill, they noticed that Mt. Hood slipped behind the trees. It was now obscured again. The forest was becoming denser as they continued their walk. Thick firs and red cedar stood everywhere. It was an old growth stand that had been unmolested for quite some time. The trees reached so high now that the sun rays barely touched the forest floors. The rays from the sun projected magnificent fingers of light through the enormous trees. Under other circumstances it would have been considered beautiful and magical by the casual viewer.

Tyler was still in the lead and the children brushed against outreached limbs in order to get through. They would stop once in a while to pull a long limb out of the way so the other could safely get through. They stepped over many dead trees that had been blown to the ground. Many of them had the bark removed so they were a bit slippery. The forest was thick and it hadn't been maimed by man. They remained quiet throughout the journey.

They stopped after a few hours of endless walking. They were exhausted. They split up their food and ate. They used their water sparingly. They were too tired to have a conversation. The sun was now behind them and it seemed to be slipping down quicker as they began their walk again. They walked for several hours more and decided to make camp for the evening. They couldn't walk any longer if they tried. Their legs ached from the long walk and their backs were strained from their backpacks.

Tyler, again, made a fire. The others to include Chloe helped pick up dead sticks, twigs, and limbs. They didn't say much as they looked at the fire, the reflection from the flames danced on their solemn and tired faces. They were covered in dirt from their endless hike and soot from the fire. They each wore new scratches from wayward limbs and brush. They each were lost in their own thought. They wanted this nightmare to be over, they wanted to go back to concrete, asphalt, and buildings. They longed for hot food and fresh water. They each knew that the water they had among them was depleting as time went on. Each step they took required additional hydration. Thankfully, Chloe carried an extra-large water container, a Dior Aqua Bottle, and she was able to distribute some water between them earlier that day. They all sat and watched the sun melt away beyond the woods. Soon after the sun completely disappeared, they were fast asleep. Jacob went to sleep as fast as the others.

In the middle of the night, Jacob woke up. He thought he had heard something. He could have sworn it was a snap of a distant limb. His compadres were sound asleep. He stoked the fire and added more wood. It was chilly, but it wasn't unbearable. He lay back down on the hard ground and fell back asleep.

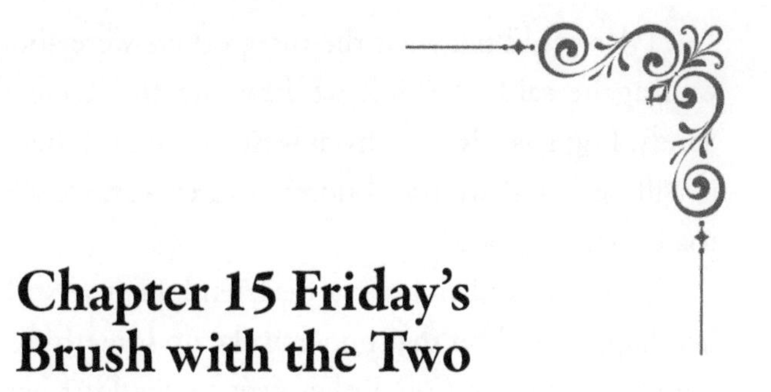

Chapter 15 Friday's Brush with the Two

Tyler was the first to be up that Friday morning. Thankfully there was no rain. The sun was beginning to make its brilliant entrance as it golden light poked through the trees. It looked almost orange. The outstretched rays painted the thin eastern clouds into a dazzling pink hue. He got the fire going again to choke out the cold morning. The others woke up with the sound of the crackling fire.

Tyler with his hands outreached above the flame, said nonchalantly, "when I went to pee, I stumbled on a forest road, about 75 yards that way." He was pointing behind them.

The four friends quickly put the fire out, stowed their ponchos, and got up. They swung their rucksacks on their back. Tyler led them to the forest road. There was a renewed sense of excitement. They were still lost in the forest, but the road offered some hope; it represented a sense of civilization.

The forest road was wide enough to accommodate a single vehicle, maybe even one large truck that hauled logs. Travelers driving through it during the wet spring had completely rutted it. There was still evidence of tire tracks, however, they were not fresh. Pockets of the road had remnants of gravel here and there. Bits of grass from the wet spring had sprouted down the middle of the dirt road. To their left, a big noble fir had fallen and now laid across the dirt road like a dead sentry. The road appeared to go from north and south from where they stood.

Tyler could tell what the three others were about to ask. Without waiting he said, "I think we head north. Remember, coming from Sandy, Highway 26 goes from west to east and then goes south. I think it will be safe if we travel north. Either way, we are now on an actual road, so that's good."

Jacob was still amazed at his friend. He was still curious as to what had happened. Did that punch wake up something inside him? Did it light some sort of fire? Either way, he couldn't have been prouder of him. Tyler stood up when he himself could not.

Without any objection, the four turned left, bounded over the fallen tree, and walked the forest road. The kids seemed to be a bit more jovial. They definitely had more energy and felt a bit more optimistic about their current plight. They each talked about what they wanted to eat when they got back. They didn't know if they could go home or if they would have to remain at the camp until it finished. Jacob silently wondered if Josh was still telling others how camp was really an undercover prison for wayward adolescents.

The road did eventually turn after around 100 yards. It took a hairpin turn to the left and also with a sudden drop in elevation. No longer heading on their desired bearing, Chloe spoke up and asked if they should turn around. The others agreed that they should stay committed to the direction they are traveling especially if they are going downhill. Somebody said that hopefully it will lead them to a paved road. A small creek eventually paralleled the road they were traveling on. The creek distanced itself from the road and the path they were on went back uphill for a countless distance. The kids continued to trudge along.

The road finally went back down in elevation. They made several dog leg and hairpin turns as they descended. As they walked further down, they noticed that there was more gravel on the road. They knew they were getting closer to a more improved road or perhaps a building. The excitement was now palpable. Chloe, Ryden, and Jacob all patted

Tyler on the back. The road was now straight for as far as they could see.

It was still mid-morning when Jacob recognized it. In the distance, about 75 to 100 yards away, Jacob could see that the road they were on intersected with another. Could it be a paved road ahead? He couldn't tell. They sped up their cadence and walked further and then they saw a car go driving by at a high rate of speed, then there was pickup, a gang of motorcycles, and then a big rig. They decided to run. It had to be the highway. They actually did it! They were once lost, but after countless miles of walking through a vast and unforgiving forest, they found their way out. This forever hike had finally found and end.

They were almost to the highway when a black Range or Land Rover driving slowly turned onto the forest road they were on. It stopped right in front of them. The bright sun created a reflection of vegetation and trees in the windshield of the vehicle. They didn't see the two occupants inside. A tall muscular man with brown hair jumped out. He had a sleeve of tattoos that ran up and down both arms. One of the tattoos looked like a bird or something with the words "Mighty Red" below it. Jacob thought to himself that they were finally saved.

"'Ello. Wha' you sconners out 'ere fer, on a 'ike, then? Lookin' fer a Camp called Pertida," said the tall man, "I think we must 'ave passed it. Can ya point us there?"

Jacob could barely understand him. He sounded English, almost like one of the band members from the Beatles. He remembered flipping through the channels once and stumbled on an interview with Paul McCartney. The stranger's words rattled out of his mouth like a gatling gun. Jacob wasn't certain where this strange man was from.

Chloe seemed to get the gist of the foreigner's words and spoke up enthusiastically. "We are from Camp Pertida!"

"So, you are. Saw you lot on the road and thou' we mus' be close. Four kiddies on a 'ike, I said to me flabby mate. You lot look quite the show! Do ye per chance to know a lad called Jacob 'art?"

He looked at all the children and vaguely recognized both Jacob and Tyler. All four kids looked dirty and disheveled. They looked like someone had dragged them over dirt and brush. One boy had two black eyes and it appeared his nose was a bit misshapen. The girl had an ugly gash above her left eye. All of them had scratches on their faces like they were attacked by a rogue wild animal. He was curious to know what this group of kids had been through. He needed to be sure that this was the boy he had been searching for.

Jacob did hear his name smothered under that thick accent. He thought the guy said lad but it sounded more like the word lid, he couldn't be sure. He rose his hand slowly like he was being called on in a class. The man slapped his own thigh with his monstrous hand and made a yelping noise of excitement. His partner seeing that he was now animated with some sort of good news immediately got out of the SUV.

"The odds. Look at that me tubby mate! The odds!" Seeing the confusion on Jacob's face he went on. "Sorry 'bout me accent, lad, I will try to speak more like a Yank, worked fer ya mum. Get excited and me accent gets the be'er of me, I mean better!" He was smiling ear to ear.

He continued, "you 'ave some'in' of mine Jacob boy, and I 'ave been searchin' 'igh and low for ya, I 'ave."

The tall man's friend remained quiet. He was much shorter than his taller companion and heavyset. His large stretched pants, that sat below a very round belly, were held up by burdened suspenders. His face was round, pockmarked, and ruddy. He almost resembled a disgruntled bulldog. He was wearing a soft brown tweed peaked cap that looked a few sizes too big. It sat askew on his fat crown covering half of his forehead and half an ear. Jacob didn't know who was more frightening the tall English man or his taciturn buddy.

Jacob was very confused, "I am sorry, sir, but I have nothing of yours."

The tall man retorted, "I think ye do, Ses'at's forbidden brush, ya nicked it at las' month's comic convention. We are going to all take a ride to git tha' brush."

Jacob wanted to make a run for it but he wasn't about to leave his three friends behind. He didn't know what to do. He kept looking back on the long road they had just traveled. He also looked at the highway. If they ran for it, could they make it to the paved road before they were caught. His friends remained quiet. Chloe and Ryden looked especially bewildered by this whole encounter.

The tall man must have been reading Jacob's mind and said, "don' ya think 'bout runnin' ya daf' boy," The man then turned to his quiet companion and gave him a nod. The short man pulled one suspender to the side showing a small pistol hidden within his elastic waistband.

"Just take me, leave my friends out of it," Jacob pleaded.

The tall man replied "no, the 'ole lot of ye, the more the merrier, g'wed, in the ba' of the Rover." He turned to his friend and said, "come on ye fat chunker, help the lovely kiddos out."

The short man opened the back door and the four children squeezed in on the tan leather seats. The inside of the Land Rover smelled a bit like bad fish and the faint aroma of warm french fries still clung in the air. The short man engaged the child's lock in both rear doors before slamming them shut.

Both men sat up front. The tall man was in the driver's seat and he was scowling at Jacob in the review mirror. He demanded to know where the brush was.

"I told you, sir, I didn't take the brush," pleaded Jacob.

The tall man started the engine, but left the vehicle in park. Still eyeing Jacob through the review mirror, the man told him about that day at the comic convention and about the brush.

He said that him and his partner, the one sitting to the right of him at that moment, had went to the comic convention that Saturday in the state capital. They had been looking for that elusive brush for almost a decade. He assured Jacob it was the real thing. It was not a fake as the vendor thought it was.

A few years ago, he and his associate had hired an actual bona fide Egyptologist to go to the vendor's comic book store in New York City to verify the authenticity of the brush. They received a tip from another associate that the item might be located at a store in New York, a store that specialized in comic books and fake Egyptian relics and memorabilia. The hired Egyptologist, a verified professional on ancient artifacts, albeit a little shady, was paid a hefty sum for this particular job. The unscrupulous authenticator traveled to an unassuming comic book store on Eckford Street in Brooklyn to examine the brush. The store was especially small and many, probably hundreds of people, walked by without ever knowing it sold comics.

The man introduced himself as an Egyptologist and professor from a local college. The greedy owner was only too happy to show him the item that he had received from his grandfather, a veteran from the Great War. The professional was allowed to make a thorough examination of it only if he remained at the store under the watchful eye of the owner. The man agreed to those conditions. It only took a few short moments with an expensive magnifying glass to reveal the genuineness of the item. He concealed his excitement from the store owner and immediately went outside the store to call the two men to confirm the brush's true authenticity. The man was then instructed to go back inside and tell the vendor that unfortunately it was a fake, which he happily did for an extra $7,000. He saw the disappointment in the owner's eyes, so he advised him to take it with him on the road at comic conventions to help drum up his business. It might be a fake but the uninitiated would never know. He added that extra advice in without any extra financial bonus.

The two men had tracked the Egyptian comic book vendor's every move waiting for a good opportunity to grab the artifact. The two men knew that the vendor from Brooklyn would be in Salem that day with the precious item in hand. On that particular day, the short man was instructed to dress in a Japanese cat costume and to start a fight with the security guard who was standing outside the enclosed Egyptian display. The muscular man joked that he couldn't believe they found a cat costume in that size. They had to special order it from Japan. In the words of the tall man, as those two were in the midst of their bleeding' tussle he was going to nick the damn brush. It would be a wonderful distraction. Unfortunately, the short man was a little too excited on his task at hand, and in haste started the brawl a bit too early, leaving little time for his partner to go and steal the precious item. By the time he got to it, it had already been stolen. The tall man, needless to say, was very dismayed that someone had the audacity to take something that didn't belong to them. He was still very upset at his portly partner for ruining the entire caper. In fact, the man said, if it wasn't for this fat jelly belly, he would be in possession of the sought-after item and he wouldn't be here ruining the children's outing.

The man also told the children about the cedar box and the Book of Thoth. It was more than evident that this man from England liked to talk and brag about his long treasure hunt for these items. The more the English man spoke the better Jacob was able to understand his accent. He got used to his unusual way of speaking. He didn't understand some of the English slang but he got the gist of it. The man told them that the brush belonged in the cedar box next to the book. In fact, there was a special pocket in the box where the brush would perfectly fit.

He and his modest associate in fact found the cedar box and the book of Thoth a few months back. Both items were found in Ohio in the study of an old rundown farm house. Those two items were later authenticated by the same Egyptologist that had validated the brush. It took him and his traveling companion ages to find the box and book. Rumors and false stories had led them all over the United States. They even flew to Alaska and once to Puerto Rico. Some stories were more plausible than others. One story in particular led them to that farm house outside of Sabina, Ohio.

Prior to ever knowing about Sabina, Ohio, the two men had stopped in San Jose, California. They heard that the objects that they were searching for could have been found by a curator who was employed by the Rosicrucian Egyptian Museum. They spoke to the director of the museum, but she emphatically denied that they had those artifacts in their possession. She also stated that it was purely speculation that they even existed in the United States. She remembered studying about those artifacts in college, but she truly believed they were still entombed or more than likely they belonged to a very wealthy collector who resided in the Middle East or perhaps Europe. She, however, did offer some additional information that would be of some interest to the two men.

She told the two men that a man had recently phoned the museum. He said his name was Heffelfinger. She couldn't forget a name like that. He told her that he had just inherited his parents' farm house in Ohio. He didn't say specifically where in Ohio. He went on to say that his mother recently passed away at the ripe age of 99. The father was unfortunately killed in action during the Second World War somewhere in Germany. Supposedly the caller didn't have a great relationship with his mother and he was quite young when his father went off to war. This gentleman explained over the phone that when he was going through the house and cataloguing the belongings, he found a cedar box that contained an old and strange looking book. The cedar box had funny writing characters on it. Part of it was made of gold. The director of the museum had offered to take a look but he never came in. She even told the man that if the item was authentic, she would reimburse him for his travel expenses. She was a skeptic and doubted that those artifacts were the real deal. The new beneficiary of the estate of his late mother only left his name. That was the last the director heard from the new owner of the Ohioan farm house.

Not believing that ancient Egyptian artifacts were really in some old farmhouse somewhere in Ohio, she never bothered to track him down.

She warned the two men that it would probably be a wild goose chase, but she reluctantly wrote down his name for them in case they forgot the name. Heffelfinger was scribbled on the back of her business card.

The men tracked down the mysterious caller who had inherited the farm house. Unfortunately, he had been very ill and died. He passed away all alone in hospice a few weeks before the men arrived to the Buckeye state. Mr. Edward S. Heffelfinger was never married and had no children of his own. As far as anyone could tell, Heffelfinger had no relatives. The house and estate were now in probate and the courts were trying to find a next of kin to take possession of the house and farmland. Without many problems or roadblocks, they were able to find the house a few short miles south of Sabina.

The residence was abandoned and by all accounts it hadn't been touched in months. It had been a beautiful house at one time. The paint was now faded and had peeled away from the siding. It was a two-story home with a wraparound porch. The front door had a special real estate lock attached to it. A "no trespassing" sign hung on the door. The two men were able to find a cellar on the backside of the home with just a small padlock on it. Busting the lock, they were able to gain access inside. The house was still furnished but it was all covered by protective sheeting. They went from room to room searching. There were really no items of interest. All the clothing, pictures, and dishes had been removed.

They found a large den in the back of the house. It was incredibly musty. There were no pictures or decorations, apart from a large bookcase, in the study. The wife must have left the room alone after her husband's death. It had a large oak desk in the middle and old leather chair. They were both covered in dust. The men searched the desk without any success. The tall man sat down in the chair and thumping his fingers on the desk he wondered where that cedar box could be hiding. They had already searched the recently deceased one room apartment.

He kept looking at the bookcase his heavyset companion was leaning against. It looked like it had been moved as it was no longer sitting up against the wall. He stood up and pulled the bookcase over spilling the old leather-bound books onto the wooden floor.

There it was, an antique cast iron safe that sat flush within the wall. It was the prettiest item in the entire decrepit house. There was an outline of where the bookcase had stood for decades. The tall man's partner had always been a successful safecracker. After retrieving some tools from their vehicle, the short man was able to open the safe with little effort.

The safe made a metallic sound indicating it was unlocked. They slowly opened the safe and there it was. The cedar box sat on the bottom shelf. It had little dust or dirt on it. In fact, it looked very clean. The black cat that was affixed to the top was still shiny. They opened the cedar box very carefully which surprisingly took more effort than opening the safe. It felt like it had been sealed shut. There sitting inside was a book just like the man who called the museum described. There was something else in the box. There was a leather-bound journal that was wrapped in leather string. They opened the front cover and it showed that the author was Mr. Henry T. Heffelfinger. This must have belonged to the father of the recently deceased the two criminals surmised. They briefly looked through the many pages. Henry had journaled about how he was able to acquire the artifacts on an adventure he took to Giza when he was a young man. It must have been 300 pages long. He had a lot to say.

After the story on how they acquired the box and the book, the man behind the steering wheel spoke again about the day at the comic convention. The tall man was in fact at the Egyptian exhibition that day when both Jacob and Tyler were there prior to the altercation. He was just a few steps from them. Of course, they wouldn't have recognized him then.

"Aww, so you were the English man dressed as the plague doctor. I knew that guy sounded like he was from England. But I thought he was a bit shorter," Jacob said interrupting the man's story. He thought it odd that there were so many British men at the comic convention.

The man in the driver's seat turned his head back to look at Jacob squarely in his face, no longer using the mirror to communicate. His face soured. In his best American accent, the man scoffed, "You damn Americans think the Brits have two accents, the Received Pronunciation accent, which is spoken by the Queen and those posh pillocks, and the Cockney accent. Truth be told, there is about 35 plus different accents across the UK. I will have you know I am from the North."

The man settled down and he continued on with his story and explained to Jacob that he was in fact not the man in the plague costume. The man in the black costume was a man named Winker. An actor in fact. After exhausting every means available, the two men were finally able to track Winker down a few weeks after the convention was over. Thankfully, the man hadn't returned to Great Britain. They found out, with the utmost certainty, it was not Mr. Winker who was in possession of the stolen brush. Having illegally obtained a list of names from the inept security guards that worked the convention that day, he was able to deduce that the other person that might have stolen it was one Jacob Hart. He remembered the boy and his little friend standing there that day eavesdropping on the conversation between the vendor and the plague doctor. Both of them were in possession of backpacks, a perfect thing to conceal stolen loot especially a brush.

Jacob remembered the name Winker. It took a second to register who the plague doctor was. It was obvious that Ethan Flynn wanted to go around and see things and enjoy the comic con without being accosted by stupid fans. He was the biggest name in Hollywood. He just wanted to be a normal guy even if it meant strolling around in costume. A pretty good disguise at that. Then all of a sudden like a punch in the gut, Jacob had a second thought.

Jacob morosely reacted, "so that's why he's been missing." He feared maybe he was more than just missing, but he didn't want to make any implications. The two men that sat in the front seat didn't look like the friendliest gentlemen. The shorter man looked like he would kill his own mother over a chicken pot pie.

Could this week get any worse? First, he was remanded to this stupid camp, made to scale down a 60-foot wall, go on a hike, get lost, only to be kidnapped by two thugs, one of whom he could barely understand, and quite likely a celebrity murderer. He never so badly wanted to be back at home. He wanted to tell his mother that he was sorry for being such a jerk for the last month. He felt he was going to lose control of his thoughts. His heart was beating faster than any track meet he had ever competed in. He couldn't slow down his racing thoughts. Each thought flew by like an out-of-control race car. His palms were sweating and his throat felt like it was collapsing. He knew he was having a panic attack. He felt detached from his body. He wanted to run. He needed to get out of the vehicle and right now wouldn't have been soon enough. He was tightly wedged in the middle between Chloe and Tyler. He had never understood claustrophobia until that very moment. It was hot inside the vehicle. Chloe must have sensed his anxiety, so she put her hand on his. Jacob thought it felt very warm. She whispered in his ear, "just breathe, Jacob."

The man didn't answer Jacob's comment, instead he asked again, "so, where is tha' bloody brush? I promise you, mate, I won't keep askin'."

Tyler, for the first time, spoke up, "he doesn't have it. It's back at my house. It doesn't belong to you; it belongs to Egypt. Just leave him alone."

The driver smiled, "well, ye right' me wee lad, it doesn't belong to me, belongs to me boss. A very wealthy collector, I might add. Paid me a bloody fortune to ge' it, the box, and the book. So, let's all take a drive back to the valley, eh? No' to worry ya lot, we will stop fer some top scran. Looks like ya lot could use it."

The road was wide but not wide enough to turn around. There was too much vegetation and trees on either side to accommodate a three-point turn. Instead, they drove up the forest road looking for a suitable turn around area. The reticent passenger up front pointed out a spot about 50 yards ahead to the right where there was a break in the tree line. The driver made the mistake of backing into the opened area and bottomed out where water had collected from the spring runoff. The area had turned into a mud pit. The vehicle sank. He placed it in four-wheel drive but unfortunately forgot to place the vehicle back into drive; the SUV was still in reverse. He turned off the stability control and with all of his force, buried the accelerator to the floor. The vehicle, with a violent jolt, shot further back lodging the rear end on top of a downed fir tree. The rear end was now off the ground and the back wheels spun helplessly. The vehicle occupants were looking out the front windshield only to see the muddy ground. The luxury vehicle was in a nose down pitch attitude. He slapped it in drive and put the vehicle in low four. The vehicle strained against the log and the front end buried itself deeper into the unforgiving sludge. Mud sprayed everywhere covering the vehicle in brown muck. He put the transmission in reverse which only made matters worse. The vehicle rocked back in forth now grappled by mud and an unyielding piece of timber.

The man slammed the vehicle back into park. With immense frustration, he said, "Right, I'll stay inside, you lot ge' ou' and push. Come on, ya overweight geezer give 'em a hand, then!"

The short man begrudgingly opened his door, slid down the right side of the passenger seat, and immediately sunk into the mud. His boots were buried, but he managed to lean forward to open the rear door. The kids, backpacks still strapped to their bodies, jumped out.

The short man didn't say anything, but motioned with both arms for the kids to get behind the vehicle to push, which they did. The man was trying hard to get to the back of the stuck vehicle. He was waddling and as he tried getting a boot out of the mud it slipped off his foot. The man tried catching his balance, he wavered for a split second, and then like a felled tree toppled over. He was face first in the mud and dirt. He grunted. That was the only sound they heard from that man that day.

The children saw their opportunity and bolted. They were too afraid to look back. Tyler tripped on another dead log just behind the pickup. Ryden stopped and yanked him up. The four ran deep into the forest only to hear a shot ring out and then another.

Chapter 16 Staff Search Party

That Friday morning, after the breakfast meal was served to the extremely quiet campers, another staff meeting was called by Ms. Holstrom. She was her usual furious self. The thin lady paced back and forth, her glasses swinging back and forth on the tethered lanyard. Her staff was waiting for her to begin a tirade for their failure in finding the lost children the day before. The air was thick with trepidation.

After several dramatic moments of silence, the thin lady finally spoke, "well, I have received a few phone calls from parents this morning. They heard we have missing children. Thankfully, these callers' children are accounted for." She glared at Nicki and then continued. "Somebody tipped them off. It was either one of you turncoats or a child with a cellphone that miraculously got a signal way out here. I told them that the situation had been handled. If the children aren't found by tonight, we will find another alternative. Don't just stand there with those dumb looks on your face, I have called in a few more people to help. GO!"

Michelle, Nicki, and the rest obviously had no success the prior day. They couldn't find a trace of evidence of the missing children. They were both sick to their stomachs. Michelle had been trained to search for people, but it was something she couldn't teach to others in such a shortened time frame. The other staff members didn't know how to properly search for lost hikers. Without the help of trained authorities, they were spinning their wheels. Michelle knew that.

Michelle gathered them up again in a classroom. She had hung a few maps on the walls. This time there were 12 staff members. Great, Nicki thought sarcastically, the extra two people will turn the tide on this ineffective hunt. All the staff members looked exhausted. None of them slept. They all looked somber and they each casted their eyes down at the floor. They understood that their efforts the day before were fruitless and today's search would probably not offer any better results.

They were all paired up again and Michelle asked them to expand their search. They were given the same items as the day before. Michelle tried her best to give them words of encouragement but that can be hard when you don't believe it yourself.

Chapter 17 Escape Friday

The four children ran for some distance keeping together. They sprinted through thick trees and vegetation. They ran through branches and thickets. They bounded over rocks and downed timber. They ran between dense sets of conifers. It was like the trees had these outstretched hands trying to slow their pace. They tripped several times over downed trees and tall vegetation, but they helped each other. They had no destination; they just knew they needed to get away from where they were. Their mouths were dry and their legs were ready to revolt from the incessant movement.

Ryden, the biggest of the four, stopped suddenly. He held his hands behind his neck like he had just finished a marathon. His face was bright red. His eyes were still puffy from the punch he had received from Tyler. He was pacing around in circles.

"I can't go on!" He emphatically said. He was panting between words. "Just, go, now, leave me, I will slow, you down." He was now bent over and he was dry heaving. "Please," he pleaded, "I will distract those bastards." Tears were flowing from his eyes, "Please. I am not a good kid anyways."

Tyler exploded, "you think we are going leave you?! After all this? You are one of us now, whether you like it or not Ryden! No, you will rest and catch your breath. That fat dude won't find us." Tyler affectionately put his hand on Ryden's back, patting it.

Chloe said, "Let's just walk, we don't need to run right now, plus we probably sound like a herd of elephants charging through the forest."

That's what they did. They walked and they did so trying to remain as quiet as possible. They avoided twigs and other noise producing objects that were on the forest floor. It was near impossible to remain soundless as they trundled through the forest. Jacob wanted to know how big animals like elk and deer foraged through the forest without making such a ruckus.

After about an hour of walking they found another creek. This one was big almost like a small river. It didn't look terribly deep. It was crystal clear and they could see the rocks settled on the bottom. It was a fresh runoff from the spring snowmelt. The moving water was freezing cold. Each child refilled their canteens and placed a tablet in it to kill the bacteria. They wanted to drink it now, but they remembered in their class that it was best to wait at least 30 minutes.

Not having an exact way to measure 30 minutes they decided to make their way downstream. They followed the creek several hundred yards. They were in thick vegetation, but they tried their best to stay on the bank. They found a safe place to cross. A large Western Hemlock had fell across the creek. Its giant roots stuck up on their side of the bank. They still had not decided on a specific destination but knew they needed to make distance between them and those evil men. They figured that being on the other side of the stream would be a good idea. They clambered on the slippery fallen tree and scampered carefully across the flowing water. They all crossed without incident.

The four continued downstream understanding that it would take them downhill. The brush and trees were getting overly dense again so they had to distance themselves from the bank of the creek.

They figured they had been walking now for well over 30 minutes. They stopped and found a large stump to sit on. They were thirsty but they knew it wouldn't be a good idea to guzzle their entire canteen. Instead, they sipped it as if it were hot tea. The water was still cold and delicious.

Jacob finally said to the group, "I am sorry I got you all wrapped up into this. This is all my fault, us getting loss, those guys are now after us."

Tyler interjected, "no, it's me who should be sorry."

Both Jacob and Tyler told the story of the events at the comic convention. Jacob told them about taking the money and sneaking away from the mall. Tyler explained about the brush and how he originally heard about it from his aunt, his mother's sister.

"It was wrong of me to take it." He was now speaking to Jacob. "I know that now, I shouldn't have jacked it. First thing I have ever swiped. This is all my fault. I jacked it when you went to the bathroom. I saw the fight and that slimy vendor next to the guard and without thinking, I just took it. Doesn't belong to me, but it don't belong to him either, or to those two men in that black SUV. It needs to go back to Egypt, where my mother's ancestors are from."

Jacob looked at him and said, "they searched your bag, man, I was there." As an afterthought, he added, "I am not sure this brush is such good luck."

"Funny thing, man, your mom got that backpack for me for Christmas last year. Remember? Well, it has a secret compartment at the bottom. I didn't know until about three months ago. I was searching for a pencil at school and I found it."

Tyler now had tears in his eyes. He went quiet. The other three were looking at him. After several moments of silence and more tears, Tyler spoke again; his voice was broken. "A little over two years ago, I was at home with my mother. My pops, he was working late. He worked a lot, you know. We lived off Fremont Street in North Portland. Small two-bedroom house. Not much to look at. We were sitting on our front porch, me and my ma. We usually liked to chill out front on our swing after dinner. She loved telling me stories. Sometimes, she would talk my ear off. I never minded. She made me laugh, always made me laugh. I remember I had a lot of iced tea at dinner that evening. We had homemade pizza. Seemed like we had the whole nine on that pizza.

Funny how you remember things like that. My mother loved making iced tea and boy, she could cook." He paused for a moment reflecting on that day.

"Anyhow, I slipped into the house real quick to use the bathroom. As I flushed the toilet, thought I heard a bunch of popping noise. Thought somebody let off a bunch of those Black Cat firecrackers. A string of 'em. I washed my hands and went into the living room. I remember everything was quiet. No more noise in the street."

Jacob didn't want to hear the rest. He was beginning to silently cry as well. He couldn't even look at Tyler now. He couldn't stand to see his best friend cry. Tyler was his only true friend; he was his brother. He knew Tyler's mother wasn't in his life, but he never wanted to ask why. Tyler never talked about her, as if she never existed. Jacob never wanted to press Tyler about his mother.

"I walked outside, my ma was on the front porch, on her hands and knees. There wasn't much blood, not like you see in the movies. Smeared blood on the wooden porch. She was gurgling though, like she was trying to talk. Crazy sound. She raised her hand to hold her throat. Tears were running down her face. I can still remember the scared look on her face, the look of panic. I remember the whole nine, man. I still see it today. It haunts me. She reached out for me and then collapsed. Never felt so helpless, never."

Tyler buried his face in both of his hands. Jacob put his arms around him. Then the other two wrapped their arms around him. They sat there for a long time in pure utter quietness. The forest, as if understanding the solemn extent of the atmosphere, went quiet.

After some time, Tyler wiped away his tears and biting his lower lip, said, "we should probably get going."

The kids picked up their belonging and trudged along. They continued walking as close to the creek as the terrain would allow. They had no words to share among each other. Only the birds in the distance, somewhere in the towering evergreens, called out piercing the deadening quiet of the forested land.

The brook meandered down the hill and finally flowed into a small lake. The lake was extremely small and it was in a shape of an elongated kidney bean. It was clear, pristine, and from the looks of it and its surroundings it had been untouched by humans. This small lake was mostly likely unnamed, but if had been named it would have been called Clear Lake. Oregon never minded having redundancies in naming bodies of water. Oregon has almost a dozen lakes officially named Clear Lake, several Elk Lakes, and two John Day Rivers, albeit one of them is a six-mile tributary near Astoria.

It was probably mid-afternoon. The four campers skirted around the dazzling lake and a few hundred yards beyond it, they spotted an old derelict cabin.

Chapter 18 Cabin in the Woods

The cabin looked abandoned. It was a single-story shanty made from old logs. It looked as if it were built when horses were still conveying people from one place to another. The entire front of the cabin had the roof extended and it pitched over the front porch. The extended roof was held up by four vertical logs. A wooden balustrade protected the front veranda. Some of the spindles had rotted out. The roof was tin and was littered with pine needles and cones. Two small front windows, both stained from dirt and age, sat on either side of the wooden door. Firewood was neatly stacked on the front porch. Vegetation had invaded the sides of the house; wild plants had fingered and crawled their way up on the outside walls. There was even an old propane tank, part of it rusted, that had been hooked up to the side of the cabin. The place was charming and a tad eerie. For some strange reason it held both qualities simultaneously, a juxtaposition of beauty and loathsomeness.

"If there is a rusted-out truck on the other side, I am bolting," said Chloe. She was trying to be humorous. Jacob looking at her thought she just didn't look right, her face seemed a bit ashen.

Ryden was perplexed and asked, "what are you talking about?"

"Oh, that's right you weren't at our campfire that night, you missed the ghost story of Old Sirus Snodgrass." Chloe tried to force a laugh but coughed instead.

Jacob, despite their current situation, felt a bit more comfortable. He didn't trust the environment he was in, but he trusted his friends. Despite the eeriness of the shelter, they had just come upon, it too offered a bit of solace.

Jacob chuckled, "Too funny, Chloe, you think some old man will answer the door wearing some old oversized coveralls? I doubt it. That cabin was supposedly at Camp Pertida. We are not anywhere near the camp. Besides, it was a just a story."

As the children walked around the cabin, surveying it like they were professional building inspectors, Chloe and Jacob took turns telling the ghost story of ol' Snodgrass. Ryden actually liked the story. They tried to be as dramatic as when Nicki told the tale but they decided she was definitely better at storytelling.

Chloe timidly asked, "do you think we should break in? Maybe there is food in there, I am not feeling very good."

Ryden replied, "It's an emergency, Chloe, if this old shack belongs to someone, they can sue Camp Pertida."

"Or my parents, they are rich enough," added Chloe. She tried to smile.

With that he tried opening the door. It was locked. He took out is knife and tried breaking the strike plate of the door frame. He put his weight into the door and after several attempts it finally broke free.

It was a one room cabin with a pantry and a large closet. The dirty small windows didn't offer much light, plus the dark wood walls made the room even more dismal. It smelled musty. Jacob almost thought he could smell the cabbage. Furniture consisted of a worn-out table with two folding metal chairs and a stripped twin size bed. The kitchen had an RV sized propane stove and a small dorm size refrigerator sitting next to it. The refrigerator must have run by propane because the cabin didn't offer electricity. On the far side of the room, a black potbelly wood stove, with four spindly legs, sat on a rocked hearth; its long black and crooked chimney poked through the ceiling. The wall was void of any pictures; however, it held some old deer antlers.

The closet was almost the size of a small bedroom but a bed would have been a tight squeeze. Instead, it held blankets, bullet reloading items, and climbing gear.

They opened the pantry door expecting to see bare shelves. It was like coming down the stairs on Christmas morning. It was fully stocked. Nuts, a sealed burlap bag of white rice, cans of sardines, several jars of honey, peanut butter, dried bags of beans, and other assorted staples of non-perishables were neatly stacked on the pantry shelves. There were even dark brown plastic packages with the words "Meals Ready to Eat" printed on them. The packages were sealed. There must have been about a dozen of them. Ryden recognized the MREs because his uncle brought them when they went hunting. The kids inventoried the loot of provisions they had just found. They brought it into the light to see if there was an expiration date on the cans and jars. It looked like everything was still edible.

"I bet this place belongs to some hunter," commented Ryden now pulling open a tin of sardines.

"We can leave a note and have them contact Camp Pertida" offered Chloe. She then coughed a little. She was sitting on the bed.

Jacob was happy to see Vienna sausages. Normally, under other circumstances back in civilization, the thought of canned wet sausages and smelly sardines would have turned his stomach. Now, these items were delicacies. They had even found several unopened gallons of drinking water.

The kids were starving. Prior to their adventure this week, only Tyler knew what it was like to be actually famished. There were many nights after his mom's funeral, that they couldn't afford to eat. His father lost his job plus his mother's funeral depleted the rest of their savings. The others three kids always had packed pantries. They probably didn't have the most ideal environment, but they always could count on sustenance.

They knew it wasn't a good idea to gorge themselves unless they wanted to be sick. It wasn't a good time to binge. It was time to try and relax and enjoy their bounty. Despite the dingy shanty they found themselves in, the place offered shelter and provided a bit of comfort.

Ryden had found a candle and ceremoniously placed it on the center of their little table. He pulled out a small lighter from his pocket and lit it.

With his mouth full of peaches, Tyler glared at Ryden and asked, "did you have that lighter this whole time?!"

Ryden shrugged and looked at Tyler mischievously. "Maybe." Then after a pregnant pause, he laughed, "no, just jacked it from a drawer." Tyler threw a plastic spoon at him.

Jacob asked what they should do after they ate. Tyler replied that they should just stay there and spend the night. There was still plenty of daylight, but they should rest and not begin a new adventure. Tyler figured that there would be a road or path near the cabin that ran back to a bigger road or the highway. They could just hang out. They could get a good night sleep and start out in the morning.

Chloe didn't seem convinced. She had her hand above her left eye where the gash was. "What about those weirdos out there? What if they find us?"

Ryden interjected, "When my uncle and I hunt, we sometimes road hunt. My uncle is a pretty big dude, he gets tired real easy. We just stay in his truck and stay on the logging roads looking for game. I think that's what these guys will do, if they have gotten their Rover unstuck. There is a lot of logging roads out there. I don't think it's a good idea to wander the forest today or tonight without a solid plan. I think Tye's right, we should just hang here. We will come up with something after resting and getting a good night sleep."

Back at Camp Pertida, Nicki, Michelle, and the ten other searchers met back up at noon as previously agreed. There was no luck. All 12 searchers were wearied and frazzled. There wasn't a scrap of evidence to bring the search party closer to their lost hikers. Dejected they returned to the cafeteria to eat and discuss their next steps.

After their quick lunch, Michelle pulled Nicki to the side. "I have had enough of this turd show, we are wasting our time, let's go."

Nicki got into Michelle's Toyota and they left. Michelle sped through the dirt and gravel road heading back to the main highway. The 4runner bounced and jolted as it traveled down the long dirt road. Both occupants, especially, Nicki held on for dear life.

"Where are we going?" Asked Nicki, bouncing on her seat holding on the vehicle's grab handle above her door.

"Those kids have been gone since Wednesday, it's now Friday. This is ridiculous. We are not professional searchers. I don't care if Betty the Vulture ever hires me again. Listen, I dated a pilot at my last duty station. Yes, fraternization, that's beside the point. She got out of the Regular Army and joined the Oregon Army National Guard. She flies for them out of Salem. They do search and rescue. I am going to get close to Government Camp and see if I can get cell service."

They finally got to the highway and made a left. As they traveled at a high rate of speed down the road a black SUV covered in dirt and mud came out of a forest road from the left and cut them off. Michelle, who was beyond upset, slammed her hand down on the horn. The driver of the black SUV rolled down his window and offered a backward V sign with his index and middle finger. Is he giving me the backward peace sign, silently asked Michelle. Then the SUV slowed down and quickly made a left and went down another forest road.

Nicki commented, "some people, huh?"

Michelle while driving was constantly looking at her phone to see if she could get a signal. After several miles of driving, she pulled over into the emergency lane and turned on her hazard lights. She was on the phone for some time telling the other person about the lost children. Michelle didn't sound like she was getting the answer she wanted. After several minutes of back and forth on the phone, she said goodbye and hung up. She looked despondent.

"Well?" Nicki anxiously asked.

"Damn red tape. I hate the government. Lesley would love to help us, but she is only a warrant officer. Her commander can't even authorize a search and rescue mission. The helicopter unit doesn't have the authority to launch a mission without the State of Oregon requesting it. She says the Clackamas County Sheriff has to call, oh, what did she say, the sheriff has to call the Office of Emergency management and request National Guard support. It has to go through several channels before that bird can even start their engines."

Nicki grabbed Michelle's phone and dialed 911. Looking over at Michelle she had tears in her eyes. "I am an idiot; I should have done this on Wednesday."

Dispatch answered and Nicki with an air of professionalism said "yes, I am Betty Holstrom, administrative director of Camp Pertida, yes off highway 26. Yes, that's right. Pertida Road, close to Forest Road 42. Yes ma'am, that's correct. We have four missing children who got lost on a hike. Yes, been gone since Wednesday. Yes, ma'am, I realize it's Friday. Can you please send the county sheriff to our location? NOW. Yes, yes, thank you. I am making the call from an associate's cell phone and I just want to let you know, I will probably lose service."

Michelle without waiting, turned around and drove back to the camp. After a few miles, she had to pull over to allow two emergency vehicles go by her. She found the turn off to Camp Pertida. This time she took her time and didn't speed. She pulled over for an unmarked grey SUV with emergency lights flashing in its grill. It flew by Michelle and Nicki.

"Guess the cavalry is here," said Nicki.

Michelle and Nicki pulled into staff parking. Several sheriff cars with their emergency lights still going were parked out in front of the lodge. A state police car pulled up and a trooper jumped out placing his blue campaign hat on his shaved head.

Several deputies, with their notepads out, were speaking to Ms. Holstrom. She had her head down looking quite ashamed. She looked up and caught the eye of Nicki as she approached her. Ms. Holstrom was telling the authorities everything she knew. It didn't sound like she was concealing any of the facts that had transpired in the last few days. She abruptly stopped her conversation with the authorities and whispered in Nicki's ear. She growled, "you and your lesbian friend can pack your bags and get off my property."

Michelle, overhearing what Ms. Holstrom said to Nicki, seethed, "listen you ugly buzzard, not until we get those kids back, I think you need as many people as you can spare to dig yourself out of the deep hole you have so elegantly thrown you and your precious owners in!"

Ms. Holstrom didn't reply. She returned to briefing the police on everything she knew about the disappearance of the campers that had been placed under her care.

A few hours later the county search and rescue team was organized and they used one of the classrooms in the lodge as the headquarters and operations center. A few minutes after that, two news stations from Portland arrived. Nicki smiled as the camera operators and reporters jumped out of the vehicle. The owners of the camp arrived shortly thereafter. Ms. Holstrom, with little fanfare and quite unceremoniously, was escorted off the premises by other staff members.

The four companions didn't do much that afternoon in their new found place. They were so tired they didn't feel like doing anything. They felt like they had been on the run for months. Chloe napped on the bed. The boys took turns going outside to make sure the men hadn't found this place.

That Friday night they brought firewood in and started a fire in the stove. They pulled the blankets from the closet for Chloe and for themselves. They ate again and with their bellies full they stretched out and slept. The floor was hard for the boys, but it was better than sleeping outside.

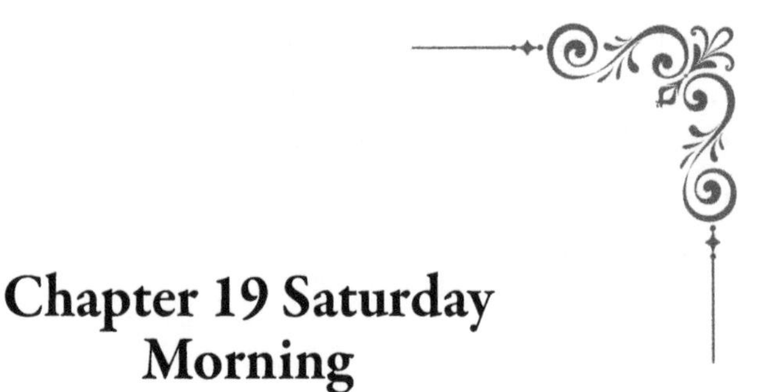

Chapter 19 Saturday Morning

Three of the four companions slept well that Friday night despite the harrowing escape they made from the two dudes. Even Jacob slept the best he had in over a week. It was Chloe that didn't sleep. She was running a fever.

The next morning the four boys snacked on canned fruit, peanut butter, and honey. They opened up another gallon of drinking water. Chloe was still in the small bed tossing and turning. The gash on her head had gotten worse. It looked like it got infected.

"What's the plan, boss?" Asked Ryden. He was speaking to Tyler.

"I don't know. I don't think we should split up. Like you said yesterday, you don't think they will go on foot to find us. Maybe we just hang out until she starts feeling better."

Jacob went back into the pantry; he was looking for something. He started taking more things out. Then he emptied the drawers in the small kitchen. He found what he was looking for. A bottle of ibuprofen. He took two pills out and helped Chloe take them. She squeezed his hand.

Ryden was snacking on a very dry poundcake he pulled out of the MRE package. He said, "I agree, we should just hang out here. If anything, we can block the door if any stranger tries to come this way. As long we stay close, maybe we can explore, you know, see if we can come up with a plan."

That Saturday morning a military Blackhawk helicopter, with red crosses plastered on both side cargo doors, was being serviced by a large white refueling truck. After the truck pulled away, the crew began starting up their helicopter. It had two pilot in the cockpit with a crew chief and a flight medic in the back. After several minutes, it took off and pointed its nose northeast and began its journey to the Mount Hood area. A few hours later it was circling around Camp Pertida.

In the cabin, the lost hikers sat there. Jacob, much to Ryden's boredom, told him about Forced Renegade. Ryden, unlike the rest of America, had never gotten into comic book films. He was busy hiding from his belligerent father. Each boy took turns sitting next to Chloe asking if she needed anything. The tablets must have helped because she was finally able to sleep. They kept a small fire going because earlier Chloe said she had chills.

Around mid-day, the boys fell asleep. They were still exhausted from the days of hiking. They no longer felt the hunger pangs. Jacob, always the light sleeper, woke up thinking he heard a helicopter fly by. It sounded really low. He didn't know if it was a dream or not. He stood up and ran out of the cabin only to see a military helicopter disappear beyond the small lake and tall trees. He woke up his friends to tell him what he saw. Tyler, sleepily, said maybe it will come back.

Back at Camp Pertida, Michelle and Nicki stayed in the classroom to offer help to the leader of the search and rescue. They wanted to go out and be on the ground, but the owners who were in the midst of a public relations nightmare, asked the two young women to help in the lodge. There was a lot to sort out.

Nicki did call Jennifer that Friday evening and told her about her missing son and his friend. Nicki felt awful and took the blame and apologized for lying to her. Jennifer liked Nicki and didn't blame her, she blamed Ms. Holstrom. Jennifer told her about the fake investigator and asked if he had anything to do with their disappearance. Nicki assured her that the kids were simply lost. No strangers ever showed up looking for her son.

The rest of the parents, those who had children that were accounted for, were all instructed to come to Camp Pertida and pick up their kids before sundown Saturday. The parents of Tyler, Chloe, and Ryden were also called that Friday night to inform them of the events. They were allowed to come in at their earliest convenience. The Portland media was anxiously waiting for the parents to be informed of the awful situation so they could release the names and hopefully the pictures of the missing adolescents on the late-night news that Friday.

Jennifer picked up Tyler's dad, Jim, and left for the mountains late that night. The other parents, being closer, had already arrived. Chloe's parents were there. They stoically stood next to their red Mercedes when they first arrived, until one of the staff members escorted them to the cafeteria. Ryden's dad was arrested shortly after he was informed that his son was missing. He got drunk, went to the nearest bar, and then proceeded to start a brawl with half the patrons and the lone bouncer. One of the unlucky patrons sustained a head injury and was taken to the hospital. Three police officers arrived and one had to use a taser to subdue him. The bail amount wouldn't be decided until the following Monday morning. The brother of the incarcerated father was asked to go to Camp Pertida in his stead, which he happily agreed to.

On Saturday, shortly after one-thirty in the afternoon, Michelle and Nicki went outside to get fresh air. The clouds closed in on the mountains and it started to drizzle. About that time, the Blackhawk landed on the backside of the lodge in the large grassy area right in front of the two women. It seemed like it took forever to shut down. The rotor blades finally came to a slow stop and both engines with a loud whine shutdown. All four crew members removed their flight helmets and climbed out of the big green helicopter and walked towards them.

Michelle recognized one of the pilots and she ran up to give her long hug. It was Lesley, a tall redheaded woman wearing a camouflaged flight suit. Next to her was the other pilot, a bald gentleman with a big friendly smile.

"Wow, Lesley, you are here! Weather not cooperating with your flight, I see," exclaimed Michelle.

"When I heard that the mission was over here, I volunteered. Yeah, the weather has us socked in. I think it will dissipate in a bit and we can re-launch. Got coffee?"

Everyone made their introductions. They were introduced to the co-pilot who went by Coop, Becky the flight medic, and a short crew chief who was called Sluggo. They made their way to the operation center.

"Wow, Michelle, this place is pretty cool. Is this a children's camp or a lodge for visiting dignitaries?" Observed Lesley.

Michelle didn't answer, instead Nicki spoke up. "So, did you guys see anything up there?" They walked through the long hallways of the lodge went into the classroom and stood next to one of the search maps. The place was still in a frenzy. People were talking on the radio, several different officers walked in and out of the room. The crew chief, Sluggo, started a conversation with one of the search and rescue leaders. He was showing the man where they had searched at.

The male pilot, Coop, turned to Michelle and said, "not as much as we would like. We tried to get as many passes before the weather decided not to play. Saw four hikers three miles east of here. They waved us off. My medic saw two unattended fires about six miles south of here. Could be someone signaling. We called that in by the way. The canopy is pretty thick though, so didn't see anyone near them. Flew as many trails as we could." He was pointing at the different locations on the map.

Nicki was very distressed and asked "did you guys see anything else?"

Lesley spoke up, "well, we did see a small cabin about 11 miles northwest of here, as the crow flies of course. We thought we saw a wisp of smoke coming out of the chimney, but the trees were so tall we couldn't get very close."

Nicki was excited, "Okay, can you point it out on the map, ma'am, please."

Lesley eyed the map for a second trying to orientate herself and then pointed in the area of the cabin. It was pretty close to a very small lake.

Nicki said, "I think I know where that is. Belongs to an old man, his name is Conners. Retired mountain guide and he used to volunteer as a technical mountain rescuer. Sort of a prepper, but a super chill guy. Comes to say hi at the end of the summer. He lives up near Seattle. Uses the cabin for hunting in the fall. Damn, I wish I had his number. Our kiddos could be there."

Lesley countered, "we just didn't think much of it, there was a black SUV, I think a Range Rover or a Land Rover, parked about 200-250 yards from it. Had a lot of mud on it. Figured the cabin belonged to the owner of the vehicle. A lot of blown down trees from the storm, maybe blocked them from going in further."

Something didn't sit right with Nicki. She kept thinking about what Lesley had said concerning the black SUV. She was trying to rack her brain. She had barely slept at all the last few nights. Why did that sound significant? She took a sip of coffee.

Michelle could see she was in deep thought and asked her friend, "what is it girl? You look like you're somewhere else."

Nicki suddenly grabbed a map and asked an officer if she could take a radio. Before he could answer, Nicki yanked it off the battery bank. Nicki grabbed Michelle and said, "we need to go, NOW."

In the hallway Jennifer and Jim were standing drinking coffee. They were given their own cabins the night before to rest in. Neither one slept and looked as haggard as Nicki. Jennifer had heavy circles under her eyes. She had no makeup on and her eyes were red from crying all night.

Jennifer grabbed Nicki by her arm and pleaded, "any updates? Please Nicki, tell me." Jennifer started balling again.

Nicki put her hand on Jennifer's shoulder and said, "maybe, but stay here. I will be back shortly. I promise"

Nicki and Michelle got in the 4runner. Michelle put her vehicle in drive and asked, "where are we going, Nick? What's going on?"

"We are heading to that cabin; I think I know how to get there."

Michelle reminded Nicki that there was a SUV parked not from the cabin. Why would the four kids be there?

Nicki told Michelle about the strange man that had showed up on Jennifer's doorstep a week prior. He had been looking for Jacob about an item that had been taken from a comic convention held in Salem last month. Jennifer was really creeped out about the encounter and then she found out he had lied about his identity.

"Okay, so?" Michelle was kindly trying to prod her friend to get to the point.

"He was driving an expensive black SUV."

Michelle slammed her hand on the steering wheel and rammed her foot into the gas pedal. "That bastard that cut us off, it was a Land Rover. He was driving in and out of forest roads like he was looking for something or somebody. It looked like it had been off roading in dirt and mud. Hang on, Nick!"

It took forever to get off Pertida Road and back on the highway despite Michelle's quick driving. The Toyota bounced back and forth hitting every rut in the road. She fishtailed around corners almost swiping the rear end of her vehicle into trees. Despite the light drizzle, a big plume of dust trailed them. Michelle, her hands tightly gripping the wheel, was steering her truck like she was in a rally race. She was fighting to keep it on the road. She didn't care.

It was Saturday and the highway was busy as vacationers traveled Oregon to camp or trek over the great Cascades. Central Oregonians wanting to escape the dry heat fled to the Ocean Beaches that were four hours away. Valley residents were headed to Central Oregon to feel the dry climate and enjoy the Junipers and desert brush landscape or perhaps to scale the basalt and tuff of Smith Rock. Traffic was heading everywhere that day. It was almost bumper to bumper.

Michelle had little patience and daringly darted onto the congested highway despite the protest of many drivers. A gentleman towing his 30-foot brand new black fifth wheel had to slam on his brakes almost losing control of his expensive camping trailer. It was close to jackknifing. Michelle threw out a consoling hand wave to make peace with the irate driver.

It was still only a two-lane highway but it didn't stop her from making illegal passes. Nicki didn't care. They would get to that cabin even if this agonizing journey killed them. They had to travel several miles on the highway until Nicki pointed out the forest road they needed to take. Michelle turned and they were almost creamed by an 18-wheeler. It laid on his big bellowing horn as they went onto the logging road.

They sped down the logging road again bouncing over the uneven terrain. It was another rutted road that curved and went up and down in elevation. There were more switchbacks that led further into the verdant forest. Nicki had only been to the cabin a few times and was trying to desperately remember which road to take. Several smaller roads branched off the road they were now on.

Michelle pulled over and took the topographic map. She had many years of experience both professionally and recreationally on land navigation. She had to take a few tests in the Army on how to navigate from one point to another using only a map, compass, and terrain association. Those tests were done on foot and she had to find at least four points in a given number of hours. There was a bit of gut instincts involved in land navigation but that was difficult to teach at leadership courses in the military. The pilot had highlighted the small lake and the approximate location of the cabin on the map. She studied it for a few moments. She then told Nicki that she thought they may have passed the road. They turned around and backtracked back to the highway to reset.

The young women pulled over near the highway intersection. They got out and changed positions. Nicki, now, in the driver's seat had Michelle take over as the navigator. Michelle told her that they couldn't speed. She needed to take time orientating the map plus this was an area that she was unfamiliar with. Smooth is slow and slow is fast Michelle explained to Nicki. She used the legend at the bottom of the map to figure out the distance between the main forest road (the one that intersected the highway) and their next turn-off. It looked like it was about two and half miles up the road on the left.

This time they slowly went down the road. Michelle noticed that there were other logging roads that weren't on the map. The map was printed only two years prior, but harvesting timber had always been big business in Oregon and new roads (that have to meet specific environmental conditions) had obviously been created to meet demand. Sometimes off roading vehicles illegally made their own new paths as well.

Michelle asked Nicki to turn on the next road. It traveled some distance deeper into dense forest. The clouds had finally dissolved and it was beginning to clear. Nicki wished she could enjoy the fresh ineffable smell of wet vegetation and timber. Perhaps she could have if it was under other conditions. She wasn't driving fast at all. A lone deer with a large antler rack, that didn't seem overly concerned about a slow approaching vehicle, stood in the center of the road in front of them. He was curiously looking at them as if wanting to know why they were in his neck of the woods. It was only at the last moment did the deer step to the side to allow the travelers to pass. The noise must have finally scared him, because he darted into the thick forest without making a sound.

The new road climbed a bit and put them at a much higher elevation. Using the hill, they were now on and spotting another hill on a ridge line to their west, Michelle was able to conclude that they were close to their destination. It was another mile or so down the road. They continued their slow drive in. They saw the parked SUV. It was the same vehicle that had cut them off. In front of it was a downed tree that was blocking the entire road.

The two women got out and looked inside the SUV. It was empty. They climbed over the big piece of timber that had toppled over the road. They stayed on the vehicle path and walked a little over 200 yards. On their left they spotted the cabin it was about 75 yards off the road. It could have been easily missed with all the vegetation and trees that surrounded it. No smoke was coming out of the chimney. It looked deserted. The back of the house faced the road and the front faced the small pond.

"Should we radio the police," asked Nicki in a whisper.

"Let's check first," replied Michelle. They tried looking through the back windows, but with all the staining and dirt they couldn't see anything. It was also just too dark inside to see anybody or even any movement.

They then circled the cabin and went to the front and onto the porch. They knocked. No answer. Then Michelle pounded on the door. The front windows, like the back, offered no evidence of occupants. They both pounded again.

Michelle cried out, "hey is there anyone in there?" No answer.

She tried opening the door, it seemed unlocked. The doorknob turned but she couldn't force it open. She didn't see a deadbolt. She rushed the door and it didn't give. It felt like something heavy was blocking it. Michelle thought she heard movement. She tried peeking into the window again.

"Let me in, or we will call the cops," yelled Michelle. She hammered on the door again with her closed fist. "Let me in, now!"

It sounded like somebody on the other side of the door was dragging items away. An eternity passed and the door opened. It was Chloe. She looked awful. Her arms were scratched up and bruised. She was dirty and her gash above her eye looked infected. She had cuts and scratches on her face.

Nicki rushed in and said, "oh my God Chloe, are you okay? Who hurt you? Where are the boys?"

Michelle was desperately searching the small cabin. She opened to look in the small closet and then the pantry.

"Please talk to me honey," demanded Nicki.

Chloe collapsed on the floor. Michelle and Nicki picked her up and gingerly placed her on the bed. She was starting to wake up.

Nicki remembered that she still had the radio. She pressed the push to talk button on the side of her radio, "help, this is Nicki Vanderworker, can you read me, anyone?"

She heard static on the radio and then she heard a male voice, "please....again....say...over."

Michell was attending to Chloe, she looked up and said, "try outside."

Nicki rushed outside towards the lake and repeated again on the radio. "Help this is Nicki Vanderworker, camp counselor at Pertida, can you hear me?"

She waited for an answer. After several agonizing moments, the radio came to life, "This is SAR Main, copy, Miss Vanderworker, we have you weak but readable, please go ahead with your traffic." Nicki had used a handheld in the past mostly when she did field work for college labs, but she wasn't quite sure about this radio lingo.

"We have located the lost female," answered Nicki. She didn't know if she was allowed to use the girl's name over the radio or not. "I repeat, we have located the lost female camper." A short pause and then she remembered to say, "over."

"Copy...your...over," said the male voice. The signal for some reason was getting worse and it was hard for Nicki to understand the radio communication. She ran back to the Cabin. She called out for Michelle.

Michelle came out. She told her that Chloe was okay, but she was too distraught to talk.

More radio static and then she heard, "please...Vander...ohv." She didn't get anything out of that transmission.

"Can you help me, I don't know how to use this damn thing, what's our location?" Nicki said to Michelle. Her frustration was palpable.

Michelle grabbed the radio. She still had the map in her hand. She got on the radio and gave them both the latitude and longitude and also the township and range of their location. There was no answer on the radio. She repeated the location again. She thought she heard the radio key up as if someone was talking, but she wasn't sure.

She looked at Nicki with a somber frown said, "I think we might have taken a radio that was still getting charged, I think the battery is about to die. I am not sure if they got our location. We should go back inside and check on Chloe."

Chloe was now sitting up on the bed. She was shaking and crying. She seemed to be in some sort of shock.

"Please talk to me Chloe, we need to find the boys. We need to also get you checked out," pleaded Nicki. She sat next to her and put her arm around her. She could feel that the young girl was burning up.

She was sobbing, but after a few moments she finally spoke, "Those two creeps, found us yesterday. I don't know what day it is. I think it was yesterday. We found the highway on our own. We hiked forever but we found the highway on our own! But they kidnapped us. They got their truck stuck and we were able to escape." She started crying again. Michelle sat on her other side. She was rubbing her back.

She continued, "we found this cabin yesterday. My head has been hurting and I just haven't felt right. I didn't sleep last night at all. My throat hurts. Jacob went outside to go the bathroom. He ran back screaming, saying those guys had found us again. The boys grabbed some rope and other stuff out of the small room. The boys had found a cliff a few miles, or yards from here. I can't remember exactly what they said. They found it last night or early this morning. I wish I could remember. It all feels like a dream. They told me to stay put and to block the doors. All three left me here. I moved everything I could against the door."

"Do you think they are heading to the cliff, Chloe?" Asked Nicki.

"I think so," answered Chloe. "Maybe they lost them there."

"Did those men ever come knock on the door?" Asked Michelle.

Chloe shook her head no and Michelle said, "they probably saw the boys and decided to go after them, they really are after something special to actually put so much effort into finding these kids, twice apparently. Those boys probably saved your life by leaving you here."

Chloe said, "they are looking for like an ancient brush, I think it belonged Cleopatra or somebody from Egypt."

Nicki had to ask, "all this nonsense, over a hair brush?"

Chloe was too sick to answer and she leaned on Nicki.

Michelle told Nicki to take Chloe and get back to the truck. She asked Nicki if she remembered how to get back to the main highway. Nicki said that she did. She didn't think she would have any problems getting back on the main highway.

"If I don't get back in 30 minutes, drive out of here, get Chloe some medical help, and call in every damn police officer you can. You have first aid training, there is a first aid kit in the way back of my 4runner. Oh, just to be safe, I have a knife in my glove compartment, slash their damn tires, all of them! Listen, Nicki, 30 minutes, not 31 minutes, got it?"

Nicki grabbed Chloe's backpack and helped her get on her feet. She looked like and felt like she lost weight. Nicki had never seen someone in such bad shape. She was covered in dirt and she looked like she had been in a fight with half of the national forest. She was unrecognizable and didn't look like the cute teenager that had lined up late for a hike just a few days ago.

Nicki walked and supported Chloe back to the waiting 4runner. It was a bit of trek because of the girl's condition. They stopped every few yards so Chloe could stop and rest. They clambered over the downed tree that was blocking the road. The black SUV was still there. Nicki got a closer look at it now. It looked two toned brown and black. The sides, from stem to stern, were painted in dried mud. She was able to open the driver's door, it was unlocked. She wanted to search it for any evidence of the lost kids, but she was hesitant to look inside. She didn't want to contaminate it if the cops decided to turn it into a crime scene. After a few seconds of contemplating, she shut the door.

She helped Chloe get into the passenger seat of the 4runner. She went to the back end of Michelle's truck and found the first aid kit. It wasn't the average first aid kit that was found in a large department store or in a car parts shop. This one was contained in an olive-green canvas backpack. It definitely must have been acquired from a medic in the Army. It was larger than an average hiking backpack. She opened it up. It folded open like a suitcase. Michelle had always amazed Nicki. She had only known her for a short time, but there was something special about Michelle. There were enough supplies in the bag to do a small surgery. There was even an IV bag in there. Nicki wished she knew how to administer fluids through a catheter. She wanted to pull out the IV kit, but instead she found some bandages, acetaminophen, and antiseptic. She grabbed the items and started treating Chloe. She was glad that she had attended the wilderness first aid classes that she was required to go to as a camp counselor. She cleaned all of her wounds taking special care of her cut above her eye.

Nicki was going to wait exactly 30 minutes. She didn't want to wait a second longer in case Chloe got worse. She was worried about the other three boys though, but she trusted Michelle. She was almost certain that Michelle would find them. Nicki sat in the driver's seat keeping a watchful eye on Chloe. 27 minutes had passed. It was like watching water boil. She started the truck and looked at her watch again. One more minute she said to Chloe even though the girl was sleeping. Hopefully the medicine was helping.

She opened the glove compartment and sitting in there was a survival knife. It was large and it was seated in a black nylon scabbard. She took it out and pulled it from its holder. It was partially serrated. Knowing Michelle, it was probably as sharp as a surgeon's scalpel. Michelle took meticulous care of everything she owned.

Taking the knife, she got out of the Toyota. She had about a minute left and she was going to leave. She plunged that knife into each tire of the muddy SUV. It felt almost cathartic as she heard the air quickly escape from the off-road tire. She stabbed each tire with an equal amount of abhorrence. If those guys came back, they weren't going anywhere.

She was returning to the 4runner and she thought she heard sirens in the distance. Maybe she was hearing things. Had Chloe turned on the radio? Was it part of a song or a commercial? She stopped. She listened. It was faint, but there were sirens somewhere beyond those trees. She quickly placed the knife back into the truck's glove compartment. Chloe was now awake. Instead of driving, Nicki ran down the road. It was a footrace. She sprinted down the road and about 200 yards she saw the lights of the first county deputy pickup. Just as she saw the truck, she heard the helicopter. It was the same Blackhawk as from earlier. The weather now clear, they were able to resume their search from the air. More emergency vehicles were on the way. The helicopter seemed to be now following the convoy of cop cars. She waved at the first pickup and motioned them to follow her back. In the chaos and excitement, she didn't think about just jumping in the truck. Instead, she ran as fast as she could back to the Toyota.

When she arrived, Chloe was outside the Toyota. She was leaning up against it. She still appeared ashen and exhausted. It looked she was winded. The deputy got out of the vehicle.

"Ms. Vanderworker?" He asked.

Nicki nodded.

"You should have told the SAR personnel where you guys were going. Thankfully the aircrew was able to tell us that you might be headed up here. We could barely hear you on the radio," said the deputy.

Nicki not knowing what to say decided to ask if there was an ambulance with them. He told them that the road was too rough and that it was waiting on the highway.

Nicki told him that Chloe needed medical attention. She didn't know how serious it was but the girl was really sick. The deputy looked at Chloe and told her everything was going to be okay. The officer got inside of his pickup and picked up his radio. With the helicopter above, Nicki couldn't hear what he was saying. He got back out. The helicopter, with the dense forest, had nowhere to land. Instead, it went up the road a short way and made a quick 180-degree turn.

The green helicopter was about 150 feet maybe 200 feet directly above them. It was hovering in one spot. Nicki could feel the downwash from the spinning rotor blades. The tops of the trees were being rustled like a storm was moving through. It was loud. The right-side cargo door on the helicopter opened up. Nicki saw the crew members in the back moving around. They both had their helmets on. One of the crew members grabbed a cable that was attached to some type of winch that was above the cargo door. One crew member with a black bag on their back, much like the one Michelle had in the rear of her truck, hooked up to the cable. It was probably the female medic Nicki met earlier at the camp. She was now hanging outside the door. The helicopter flew forward several feet and stopped to a hover. The medic gave the crew chief a thumbs up. The crew chief had some sort of controller in his hand. The medic was now descending down the cable as the helicopter stayed hovering in one place. In just a few short seconds the medic landed like a feather on the road on the other side of the downed log. She unclipped and walked over back towards the vehicles. The cable was reeled back up into the winch. For some unknown reason, the helicopter departed. The wind and the loud sound was gone.

The medic introduced herself to Chloe. She said her name was Becky. She said she was a paramedic. When she wasn't flying in helicopters for the National Guard, she was a firefighter for Portland Fire and Rescue. She was extremely friendly and continued to smile. She took off her flight gloves and replaced them with blue medical gloves. Becky asked her old she was. Chloe replied that she would be 13 in a few days. She wished her a happy birthday. Becky told her that she has a little sister that was also 13. She opened her medic bag and removed a few medical instruments. She began doing an assessment on Chloe. She checked her temperature and the rest of her vital signs. Becky walked over to Nicki and the deputy and said that she thought Chloe was stable but she felt it would be a good idea to get her on the helicopter and at least get her to a waiting ambulance. She was dehydrated and had a fever mostly like from an infection and being exposed to the different temperatures. Becky also said they might have to go get fuel after that but they would be back to help search for the rest of the kids.

Becky got on her radio and said, "Guard Copter 982, I am ready for pickup with one patient, stable, and ambulatory, over."

The crew on the helicopter asked if they needed the stokes basket dropped down.

"Negative, no stokes, requesting a patient harness, over."

Chloe gave Nicki a hug. She whispered into Nicki's ear and told her thanks and also to tell the boys that she missed them terribly, especially Jacob.

In a few minutes the helicopter returned. The medic had walked Chloe back over to where she had initially been dropped down. The helicopter with the cargo door opened and moved, now over their position. The cable dropped. It had a red harness attached to it. The medic picked up the cable. She wrapped the harness around Chloe. She attached her and her patient to the cable and then wrapped her arms around Chloe. The medic looked up at the waiting crew chief and gave him a thumbs up. They were both lifted off the road. Chloe was inside the bird in a few seconds. The cargo door closed and after a few moments, the helicopter flew away. The whole thing was a spectacular site. Nicki was impressed with the whole helicopter ordeal. She said to herself, one down and three to go.

Nicki spoke to the deputy and the state patrolmen who arrived. She told them everything she knew. She explained to them about the two men and their black SUV. She told them about the encounter they had with Jennifer and also what Chloe told them earlier. She told them that Michelle was now looking for the boys. She assured the officers that Michelle knew what she was doing. She explained to them that she was an experienced combat veteran who had been in worse situations. She also told them that Chloe thought that the boys would be heading to a nearby cliff to try and lose them. With Chloe on her way to safety and getting treated by medical personnel, Nicki thought it would be best to stay there near the cabin. She wanted to make sure the rest of her kids were going to be okay.

The deputy called in to dispatch to have a search party team meet them at their current location. He wanted the operations center to be moved here close to the SUV. Hopefully they had closed the search size to just this area. They hoped the kids weren't too far away. He also ordered a police emergency response team that was made up of specially trained officers from the Portland area. He also wanted additional canine teams to see if they could get a scent off the SUV and then search for the men. The state police called and asked for the FBI considering the circumstances of their situation and a possible kidnapping. This was going to be an all-out search until those kids were found safely.

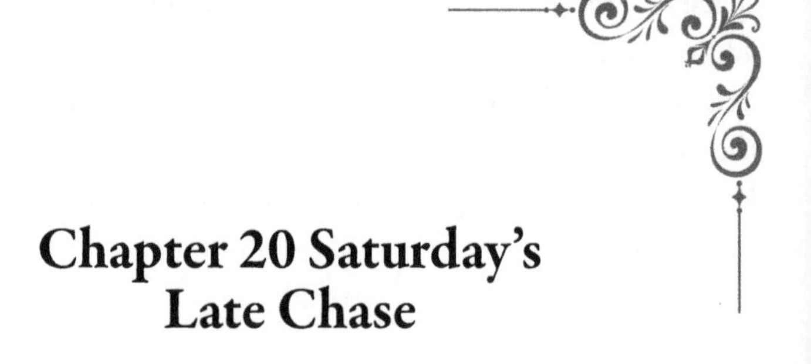

Chapter 20 Saturday's Late Chase

When Michelle left Nicki, she raced to the cliff with map in hand. Hopefully it was the same cliff Chloe had mentioned. It wasn't too far from the cabin, maybe a half mile away. The small river went in that direction so she used that as a marker for her heading. After a short distance and little time, she found the cliff. She had to search to see where the boys might have gone over. It would have been smart of the boys if they had tried using the cliff as a rappelling tower so they could get away from the men. She figured they went over the cliff on this side of the creek. She looked around and found what she was looking for. There were three different ropes still secured to three different trees.

She looked down and saw that the bottom was maybe 100 to 125 feet down. She figured that those must be some long climbing ropes. She heard the water crashing down below.

She didn't have time to make a seated harness nor did she have any climbing carabiners. She would have to hold onto the rope without gloves and hope for the best. She grabbed one of the ropes and started climbing down. It was a sheer cliff. There was no angle to it and an unfortunate fall at this height would result in certain death. There was no doubt about that.

Michelle, before she joined the Army, was deathly afraid of heights. One early evening when she 15, a friend dared her to go on the roof of her own house. She had to convince herself to climb the rickety wooden ladder that was leaning up against the home. Her father had been using it to repaint. Michelle finally found the courage to get on the roof and her friend soon joined her. Her friend brought a portable radio. They listened to music until the sun went down. When it was time to get off the roof, Michelle missed the first step of the ladder and fell onto the pavement below. She broke both of her arms and received a concussion. Michelle's mother was working the late shift. Michelle remembered that her father wasn't too pleased to have to take her to the emergency room during his Monday night football game. His Seahawks were down by three.

When Michelle was in basic training, she was going to quit on the day all the recruits had to go to the confidence course. One structure they had to conquer towards the end of their basic training was called Victory Tower. It was 40 feet tall. She remembered crying. One of the drill sergeants pulled her aside and told her that it was now or never. If she was going to give up so easily inside her head, then she would give up easily on everything else that life threw at her. Michelle became determined and she climbed that tower that day. She didn't enjoy it, but she did it. It was one of her finest accomplishments in her life. If she could scale a 40-foot tower, then she could rappel out of helicopter, crew a Blackhawk in a combat zone, and now, chase bad guys through the forest and find those boys. She was still scared of heights but she used it as a catalyst to move forward. She always thought it was the people that had no fear that were the most dangerous. When she was an instructor at the air assault school, she would tell the students when they were on top of the tower, "be brave now, when you are back on the ground, then you have time to be scared."

It took time to scale down that cliff. She had to use her upper body strength to keep herself from falling and she used the crevices to plant her feet. She finally found the bottom of that tall cliff. Where now, she pondered. Clouds had formed and it was threatening to rain. The waterfall wasn't very far from her. The mountain water angrily rushed over the precipice and came crashing down onto waiting rocks creating a plume of white wash. The noise was loud, almost deafening. The water settled beyond the rocks and it created a nice pool.

She thought she heard a helicopter nearby but she wasn't certain. Hopefully Chloe was getting the medical help she needed either way. The thirty minutes that she gave Nicki had passed. She decided it was best to follow the river and the hiking trail that was next to it. Hopefully the boys decided to follow the river downstream.

She walked for a few miles. The hiking path was nice and wide that paralleled the river. She didn't notice anything unusual. This area would be quite the hike in for a novice hiker so she wasn't surprised that there weren't any people out here. She estimated that the trailhead was probably 18 to 20 miles away at least. And it ended near the waterfall. She wasn't certain if the two guys would have actually scaled down those ropes. If they weren't experienced, they probably didn't go down them, instead they would have found another way. She didn't think the average person would scale down or rappel down without at least a little training. If those men went around then the boys bought themselves a lot of time. She had to hand it those boys and she smiled thinking about the training she put them through just a few days prior. She had met Ryden during her class and she thought he was a bit of a bully, but she really liked Tyler and Jacob.

She decided to run the trail. The clouds were now even thicker and the sky began to spit rain. You have to love Oregon she thought. The calendar could never be bothered to tell the Oregon weather what the month and day were. She had just completed a marathon this past spring in Bend and she had the energy and stamina to follow this trail to the end. Again, she hoped the boys had the same plan of using the river and the path as a way out.

She kept an easy pace as she didn't want to burn herself out. She always watched in amazement at fun runs where people would go racing out of the gate like they were strapped to a rocket. Then three to five miles down the road they were often already walking or at least slowed to a tepid jog. Yes, the tortoise can often win the race. This race she was now doing, would be downhill and she didn't need to weave in between runners with dogs and strollers.

After three or four miles, she didn't know because she didn't think about starting her running watch, she thought she heard rustling in the trees. She stopped in her tracks. She turned to her right. She yelled out. The forest was dense and she couldn't see very far into the tree stand.

"Hey, is there anyone there?" She waited. Then again, she yelled, "hello, is there anyone out there?"

After a few minutes, she heard the rustling of brush, the snapping of limbs, and crunching of the forest floor. A big boy with two dark black eyes and a deformed looking nose jumped out onto the path. It took a second for Michelle to recognize him.

"Ryden, is that you? You scared the bajeezus out of me." Michelle was taken aback. "Are you okay, where's Tyler and Jacob?"

"I couldn't keep up with them. I was out of breath. I told them to go ahead, that I was only slowing them down. They didn't want to leave me. That's what I get for being fat." The boy started crying. He continued. "I ran into the forest. They were going to stay on this path and see if they could find the trailhead. They were sure they could keep ahead of them two jerks. I should have stayed with them, huh?"

Michelle gave the boy a long hug and said, "no, you helped them Ryden. What you did was brave. Did those men come by yet?"

Ryden answered, "yes, you missed them by, I don't know, 15 or 20 minutes, I think. I heard them go by. The tall man was yelling at his buddy. Kept calling him a fat and stupid, I think he was saying pillock? It's hard understanding those British guys. Told him that it was his fault that they were in this mess."

"And Tyler and Jacob? How far do you think they are in front of those guys?"

"I just don't know. They might be 20 minutes in front of them, maybe 30 minutes. I don't know if the men scaled down the cliff or went around. I don't have a watch. I have been hiding in these woods for, I don't know, forever."

"It's okay Ryden. I am going to find them. You are going to follow this path back upstream and wait at the waterfall. Wait there! Nicki went to go get help, so I am hoping there will be search and rescue team there soon. You tell them where you met me, where the boys are headed, and how far the men are behind them. You tell them everything. Everything, Ryden. We need all the help we can get."

Ryden was nodding his head, wiping his tears with his hands, and then he asked, "is Chloe going to be okay?"

Michelle said Chloe was with Nicki when she last saw her. She was going to be okay. Hopefully she was getting medical treatment. Michelle again told him to head back upstream and not to get off the trail. He reached out and gave her a hug and left. Michelle watched him trot off until he disappeared around a bend. She could not be certain if that was the same boy she had encountered during her rappelling class just a few day prior. Then he was tripping the other boys or purposefully bumping into them. He had changed somehow.

Michelle continued downstream again. The rain was now coming down in torrents. She didn't think helicopters would launch with the weather. She decided to jog again and see if she could catch up with them. She didn't know what she would do if she encountered the men. She was hoping she could sneak around them and catch up to the boys.

Much to her surprise she indeed found the two men on the path. They were probably 50 yards in front of her. Michelle remained quiet. Every time she thought they would turn around, she would duck behind a tree. One tall muscular man and one short man. They were walking slow. The short man was trying his best to keep up but he didn't have the legs to pace with his friend. It looked like the shorter of the two was limping a bit as the taller one was yelling at him. The rushing water was drowning out their conversation.

Michelle decided to go deep into the woods and skirt around them. She didn't want to be noticed by those two. She walked into the dense forest. A few years before she went to Afghanistan her aviation unit required her to attend SERE training at Fort Bragg. It was roughly three weeks longs. Survival, evasion, resistance, and escape. It was a tough but fun school for Michelle. She learned to survive on food found in Mother Nature. She also learned how to make a shelter just using what she could find. More importantly she learned how to move from one place to another without being caught by the bad guys. She was hoping her training would pay off as she walked through the woods.

Time had slipped away quickly and it was no longer on her side. She looked down at her watch. She was surprised to learn that it was after six. How long as she been chasing these boys for? It was still raining, soaking her clothes and the ground. She had been on this trail for an unknown amount of time. She had just under three hours of reasonable light. She was thinking that sunset was going to be close to nine that night. The summer solstice was just around the corner.

She traveled in the dense woods for quite a distance. She ran and walked. She didn't want to trip over anything as she went through the thick vegetation. The rain had caused the ground to be slick. She was very certain that the distance she had covered, she had passed the two men on the trail. She decided to cut back over to the river. It took her a little time, but she found the trail without any problems. She figured that she was way ahead of the two men. Her map told her the river she was next to was named Lost Creek. She thought that was fitting. The creek was growing wider the further downstream she went.

She heard movement up ahead. She decided to run. She was tired but she had enough stamina to continue. She ran for almost a mile. If it was the boys, they were probably running. Up ahead, the path was blocked by several downed trees. Part of the trees had landed into the rushing water creating white water rapids. The downed timber was massive so Michelle decided to go around them.

She went to into the woods a bit to bypass the fallen wood and looked around. It was an old growth area. It was a thick grove of fir trees. She saw and heard movement up ahead. Limbs from the firs had been disturbed. She could see the broken branches. Maybe it was just an animal making its way through the timber. She thought she saw somebody, but she wasn't quite sure. She quietly walked towards where heard the sound had come from. The rain dripped off the trees. It was nasty weather.

Ahead in the distance she recognized the camouflaged poncho up against the tree. This was one the camp let the kids use. The ponchos always reminded Michelle of something the military had issued only this one was nicer. Military cold and wet weather items were often called snivel gear by the Soldiers. The camp's item was a cross between a nice waterproof field blanket and a poncho. The Army issued a poncho and a military poncho liner separately. They were two different items that the soldier was responsible for. Soldiers affectionally called the camouflaged liners a woobie. The woobie wasn't meant to keep the rain off you, just to keep you warm. Soldiers usually used their woobie when they slept in the field. Michelle even slept with hers when she was in garrison. The true military olive drab poncho kept the rain off, but it didn't offer too much warmth. That's what Gortex was for. Michelle always laughed or smirked when she saw a commercial that advertised that the item was "military grade." Didn't people know that the government buys from the lowest bidder? This poncho, however, up against the tree was a quality item. This was high quality snivel gear.

She grabbed it. There was nothing under it. They must have just left. The movement she saw wasn't just caused by a poncho that laid up against a tree. She looked around and it felt like someone was watching her. She called out. The men were quite aways away, but she didn't want to be too loud. She looked around to see if she could find any evidence of where they might have gone.

"Hey, who's there? It's Michelle," she softly cried out. The rain was still coming down but it was warm. The rain was lessening and turning into a summer drizzle.

She waited in silence and then after a few moments, she called out again. This time there was a rustle behind the evergreens up ahead.

"It's okay, I am by myself. It's okay, I promise," pleaded Michelle.

Then like two ghosts, Tyler and Jacob emerged from behind a tree. They both looked awful. They had scratches on their face and on their arms. They were covered in dirt. Even the rain couldn't wash off their smeared muck. Michelle hardly recognized them. They both looked pitiful like drowned rats. Jacob was limping and he was holding his right arm. His blonde hair was soaked. His arm looked as if it was broken. The two boys seemed unsure and it was like they didn't trust their eyes or didn't trust the person in front of them.

Michelle rushed up to them. She gave Tyler a hug and wrapped her arm around Jacob's right side. They didn't say anything. They were in shock.

"Oh, my goodness, boys. What happened to your arm, Jacob? You both look awful."

Jacob had a vacant look in his eyes and he didn't respond. It looked like he was somewhere else. He was in trance. The rain was still dripping off his blonde matted hair and onto his face. He had a yellow bruise on the center of his forehead.

Tyler answered for him. "He tried jumping over a tree, slipped, and fell."

Michelle then asked what had happened at the cabin.

Tyler tried explaining everything to her. All four of them were in the cabin earlier. They didn't have much of a plan yet, so they decided to stay put. Chloe was pretty sick. They didn't think it would be a good idea to move her as she was running a fever again. She was talking in her sleep. They figured she got sick from her injuries and being outside for a few days in both the heat and the cold. Jacob had gone outside for a few minutes and he came running back inside. He was screaming that those two guys showed up. He saw their black Rover. The three boys, to get fresh air, had earlier scouted out a cliff nearby. They grabbed the ropes and carabiners from the closet. They told Chloe to block the door with everything she could. Ryden saw the two men and yelled at them and he even threw a few rocks at them. He wanted to keep them away from Chloe and the cabin. The men gave chase, but the boys were much faster and were able to get a good distance between them. The boys were able tie their ropes to the trees to use as sold anchors. They even quickly made Swiss Seats and rappelled down to the bottom of the tall cliff.

They reached the ground without any problems other than slamming into the rocks that jutted out from the cliff.. They saw the trail that was near the waterfall. They all decided to use it thinking it would lead to a trailhead somewhere in the distance. The small river and the waterfall were both spectacular and they were surprised that they didn't see any hikers even if the weather wasn't great.

It was true that the managers of the forest didn't want this area too well advertised. It was memorizing with the surrounding vegetation, the clear rushing water as it wound its way over jutted rocks and downed tree, and of course the postcard waterfall. It was the essence of Oregon's beauty and the less people knew about it, the better. The clouds and rain actually added to its magic and charm. The tragic irony of people is they have a loathsome habit of blindly destroying the things that they most cherish. The forestry department kept the trail off most recreational maps. Because of the length of the trail, only the most devoted hikers ventured this far in. It would be rare to see someone here in the deep forest of Oregon.

The boys hadn't realized that the trail began 20 miles from the waterfall. They ran that trail as fast as they could. The path because of its location so deep into the wilderness, wasn't well maintained. The rain came from nowhere. It didn't help their journey as it made everything slippery. They jumped over downed wood, rocks, and overgrown vegetation. They didn't know if the men would use the rope to scale down the cliff or not. They didn't want to stop to find out how close they were. After a while of running, Ryden stopped and pleaded with them to leave him. He couldn't breathe and his legs were cramped. They all argued, but they agreed that the men weren't after Ryden. He said he would go into the tree line to keep out of the men's view.

The boys reluctantly left Ryden and went ahead still following the trail and the small river. The big rain drops plopped into the river making massive splashes. They were also tired and couldn't maintain the pace they had before. They hoped that they had a big distance between them and the chasing men. They had to conserve as much energy as they could. The found the large downed trees that blocked the trail and went into the river. The planned on getting off the trail and try and box around the impasse. They thought they had heard movement behind them. They were surprised that the two men had caught up to them. The shorter man didn't seem like he was in very good shape. They didn't want to take any chances so they went deeper into the forest. When Jacob was going over a fallen piece of timber, he slipped and broke his arm.

"I am so sorry, Jacob. It was me that you heard," said Michelle. She felt awful that she had caused his injury.

"Ryden is safe, I ran into him. I told him to head back to the waterfall. Chloe is also safe. She is with Nicki. Listen, I know you are hurt, Jacob, but we have to make it back to the waterfall. This trail that goes next to the river, it's too long. It would take forever to get to the road. With your injury it's a better idea to head back to the waterfall. Nicki would have called in the entire police force, so they are near the cabin looking for us. And with luck they are heading this way."

Jacob was still silent. Tyler said, "those guys are between us and the waterfall."

"You are correct Tyler. We can go around them. They are going to stay on the trail. I don't think they can navigate inside the forest. I can though. Either way, we can't stay here. We have to move." She was looking at Jacob. "You can do this, Jacob. I know you can, you're the toughest kid I have ever met."

Tyler asked, "can we make it Michelle? I mean before the sun goes down. There isn't a lot of light yet."

"You're right, I don't think so. But we can get close and finish the remainder in the morning. I am hoping the search party is headed this way."

Michelle thought to herself that no matter which direction they headed, the descending sun, covered by clouds or not, would do them no favors that evening.

With Michelle in the lead, they headed back to the waterfall. They kept deep in the forest. Michelle's compass was still in her truck so she had to rely on her instinct and the clouded sun to head in the right direction. It was going to be a long walk back. It was getting dark fast. The rain finally stopped, but the clouds remained and didn't allow much light. They walked as far as they could and stopped a little after nine that evening. It was too dark to travel. Besides the kids needed to rest. Michelle could have continued to walk, but she didn't think it would have been a good idea with the two boys.

They found a secluded spot among the tall timber. They agreed to try and stay awake as long as possible. Michelle felt the exhaustion that swept over her. They couldn't keep their eyes open so they all fell asleep in about 30 minutes.

Michelle woke up to the smell of smoke. It was still pitch black. With her eyes closed a chill ran down her spine. She slowly opened her eyes to see there was small camp fire next to them. Tyler and Jacob were awake. Michelle tried stomping it out, but because of the heat she couldn't. There were too many flames and red coals. She then tried kicking it out and that too had little success.

She said in a low whisper, "you can't do that, they could find us. The smell of smoke travels too far."

Tyler looked at her and then he looked at his friend. Tyler replied, "I don't think Jacob is doing too well. He is shivering. I don't care if we get caught. Jacob needs help. He hasn't said anything in long time."

"You don't mind if we join your fire, then?"

Chapter 21 Camp Pertida

Even though Chloe was quite ill, she enjoyed her first helicopter ride. She knew her dad sometimes got to ride on helicopters for his work but she never had the opportunity. Becky administered an IV into her arm when they were flying. They dropped her off at Government camp where an ambulance was waiting. She gave Becky a hug and thanked her. The ambulance took her into Gresham and she was treated at the hospital. She was given more medicine and an additional IV. She was extremely dehydrated. Her parents met her there.

The doctor recommended that her parents take her home. Home would be a better place to recover. Her doctor believed that sometimes hospitals could make people more ill. At times it was better to treat people at hospitals with injuries instead of illnesses the doctor said. The doctor told her parents to have her see her pediatrician the following Monday.

Chloe was placed in a wheelchair and rolled to her mom's Mercedes. Chloe was quite resilient and when she climbed in the back of her mom's luxury sedan, she insisted that they head back to Camp Pertida. Her father had always been stoic and his expression never wavered. Her mother immediately objected to her foolish thinking. She assured her daughter that she wasn't thinking straight. They were going to head back to their house next to the lake so she could recover from her ordeal.

"Chloe, you just got released from the hospital after being lost in the woods for half a week. We are heading home young lady and there will be no further discussion," her mother exclaimed.

There was immediate silence inside the car. The silence was thundering and it permeated throughout the luxury car with its leather seats. Chloe could no longer contain herself and seethed, "Listen, the way you treat me, the way you ignore me and look at me like I am a burden or some sort of consolation prize, I don't know which, it has to stop. I am not sure what I did to you both. Am I not good enough? Sorry I am not the expensive accessory that you would like me to be! Sorry, mother, can't be your Hermes Birkin Handbag. If you do one thing, one thing in your life, you can take me back to Camp Pertida. My friends, the ones that have spent more time with me than either of you, are missing and I am not going to go back home and wonder if they are okay!"

Her father didn't say anything. He put his wife's car in drive and headed back up the mountain. Her mother just stared out the window so she could hide her tears.

They made it back to Camp Pertida late that evening. The owners were surprised that they had returned but they understood that Chloe was worried about her friends. They would be welcome to stay as long as they so desired. Besides, it was only known to her parents and the owners, that Chloe's dad had invested quite a sum of money into this camp.

Ryden was there in the cafeteria sitting between his aunt and uncle. He had white bandages on his nose. His uncle was a jovial looking man. He had a scruffy beard and wore a big trucker's hat. He had his thick arm around his nephew. Every so often he would kiss him on the top of his head.

Michelle was absolutely correct. There were several deputies that Ryden ran into way before he found the waterfall. He told the deputies everything he knew. One escorted him back to the operations center next to the cabin. A medic on sight treated him and gave him an IV. After the medic was done, a state police officer drove him back to camp to be reunited with his aunt and uncle.

Chloe gave Ryden a big hug when she saw him. He was still wearing his Yankee baseball cap. She started crying again. Ryden and his aunt and uncle were going to stay the night and wait until the boys came back. The owners didn't want to turn any campers or their parents away.

At the other end of the cafeteria, there were two people sitting next to each other. A man and a woman. Chloe knew it had to be Jacob and Tyler's parents. She walked up to them. She introduced herself. She told them both that their boys would be forever her best friends. Jennifer reached out her hand and squeezed it. Chloe told them everything from the day they left for the hike. She explained to them how brave their boys were. Jim stood up, took off his hat, and gave Chloe a hug. He thanked her for everything. Chloe stood there weeping.

Chapter 22 Captured, Again

They turned around to see the tall man and his short companion. They stood there looking like two ghosts. They must have been there for some time. Just waiting for the right time to make their grand entrance.

"Fancy to find you lot out here. Looks like you lads lost two of your mates and gained a nice-lookin' bird," sneered the taller man.

Michelle immediately stood up and struck the man with a closed fist. Even though she had stepped into her punch, it had not fazed the man. He replied with a smile.

"That all you got, duck? You got spunk, love." He wiped his chin with his hand. He had a backpack in his hand. It looked like it belonged to Tyler. "Found this on the trail, still has some rope in it."

He turned to his short friend and said, "okay ya daft git, tie 'em up. Be useful. Do I have to do all the work?"

The short man gathered the captives and escorted them to a nearby tree. The diameter of it must have been at least five feet.

While the three captives were being tied up, the tattooed man spoke, "so, I 'aven't properly introduced us. Name is Alpine. My little well-fed mate 'ere is named Lowland, innit? You guys took off, yesterday, before I could tell ya. You guys really played my nerves. Been all over the woods looking for ya. Don't care to see another tree for the rest of me life. We are going to wait 'til daylight, head back to the Rover and we are going to get tha' brush. No more funny business. I am a little knackered, and my chubby little mate probably needs a large pizza to himself followed by a long sooty."

As the man gave his speech, Tyler told the short man to be careful with Jacob's arm. They were all tied to the large fir with the rope tight around their torsos; they wouldn't be going anywhere.

Michelle glared at the two men as they warmed themselves by the fire. She had always been full of venom. It got her in trouble on more than once occasion. She was the only soldier that she knew that had got promoted to Private First Class twice. She still had that article 15 framed on her wall. It was a badge of honor.

She remembered the events like they were yesterday. One afternoon she was in the hangar replacing a starter on a Blackhawk. She was covered in grime. This was well before she became a crew chief. A young male sergeant from another platoon walked up and told her that she had no business being an aircraft mechanic. He said that he was glad that he didn't have to ride on the bird she was working on. He wished that women stayed in the medical field or did administrative duties. They had no business being outside the wire. The man harassed her for weeks. He even followed her to the dining facility and then to her barracks. She tried telling her chain of command, but they told her not worry about it.

One night she left the NCO club, she was by herself and she was walking back to her room. He was there standing on the sidewalk blocking her path. He had a wicked smile on his face. He tried grabbing her, but she quickly moved to the side and punched him several times, eventually knocking him down. The MPs were just driving by and witnessed the end of the scuffle. She was on top of him with both of her fist raining down on his bleeding face. She was apprehended for assault, placed in back of the patrol car, and detained at the MP station. The sergeant was sent to the hospital to be treated for a concussion, broken nose, and numerous lacerations. Her first sergeant, the highest-ranking enlisted Soldier in her unit, came to pick her up from the station.

The first sergeant was sympathetic to her story and recommend a light punishment for her actions. However, with the military policeman's detailed statement and the statement from the injured NCO, who was her senior, her case was pretty much indefensible. Her commander reduced her in rank and took away her pay for half a month. He said that the incident with the sergeant could have been handled without resorting to violence. She wholeheartedly agreed. The injured sergeant, after recovering from his injuries and getting promoted to staff sergeant, was moved to a different unit.

Michelle thought about her past as she sat there tied up to the tree.

Michelle couldn't contain herself any longer and vehemently said, "you two think you are just going to walk back to the cabin?"

She started to laugh. "Do you think I just appeared from outer space? Where do you think I came from? You idiots, that entire cabin and the surrounding area is surrounded by police. Half of Oregon's law enforcement are there. Chloe, their friend. Did you meet her? Sweet girl. Her parents donated a million dollars to the Governor for her campaign. I won't be surprised if the FBI is on their way here."

Tyler could read the man's face, the one who called himself, Alpine. He looked like he was going to have an aneurism. Tyler spoke up, "I bet you had something special in that black truck of yours, you sure ain't carrying it with you."

Alpine's face flushed. The man turned to his companion and exploded, "Lowland, ya dumb muppet, I told you, you should 'ave stayed in the Rover. You 'ad to follow me, didn't ya?!"

Michelle was talking to the tall man and said, "I think you are the dumb, what did you say? Muppet."

Alpine bent down over her and without saying a word backhanded her across the face. The slap was loud and any louder and it would have echoed through the dark forest. She didn't say a word. She turned her head and spit out a little trace of blood.

"That all you got?" She was smiling and then she added, "Duck!"

He didn't respond. Instead, he turned to his friend, Lowland. "All this work. Fer nothin'." He picked up a limb and flung it at a tree. "What we gunna do, mate?"

Alpine and his taciturn partner sat down next to the fire. Alpine said, "can't go back to the bloody Rover. We should probably head away from 'ere at daybreak. We have the whole bleedin' state lookin' for us. This lot, they are going to slow us down. Say we get out a 'ere and head west. That sea captain in Astoria, his name's Labaree, innit? We done a few deals with tha' bloke. See if we can catch a ship back to Blighty. We are done here. Bad luck the entire thing. I reckon we ran out of options, hadn't we?"

He leaned closer to his partner and whispered in a low voice. "If it weren't for 'em kids we would be sitting on a fortune. We don't need 'em around, if you catch me drift. Less witnesses the be'er. Wait 'til morning, they can sweat on it 'til then. One more thing, if you weren't me dumb brother, I would kill you meself."

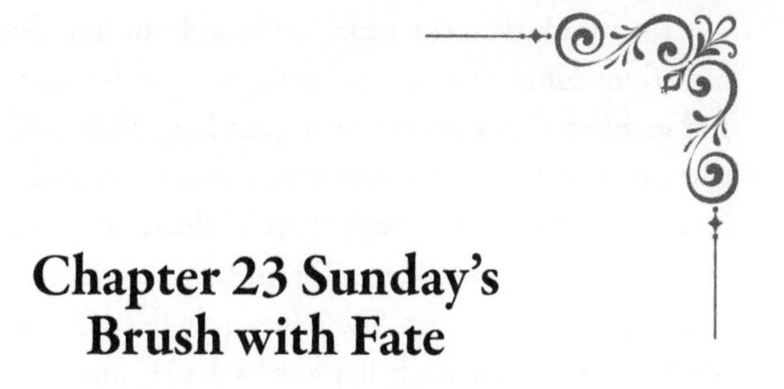

Chapter 23 Sunday's Brush with Fate

Chloe woke up well before her parents. She was still weak but felt much better than she had. She snuck out of the cabin and went into Cabin B. The sun still wasn't up. Thankfully the door was unlocked. The lights in the cabin were out. The cabin had been vacated for a few days and all the beds had been stripped except for Tyler's and Jacob's. The children had written cards to the missing boys and placed them on both of their beds.

Tyler's wall locker was still closed and locked. She took out a wadded yellow piece of paper and looked at it. She unlocked the combination and opened his locker. The wall locker didn't have much in it. It was almost empty. She moved some clothes and socks around. There it was at the bottom. It was wrapped in old cloth. She methodically opened it up and it was just as described. It looked very old. She was holding something that was made over 3,000 years ago. She rolled it over in her hand. It felt weird to hold onto it. She quickly wrapped it back up and placed it in her bag.

She went back to the cabin where she stayed with her parents. Her dad was awake. He had just gotten dressed as he could no longer sleep. He gave her a long hug and apologized. He said there would be some changes when this was all over. She thanked him and then she asked if he would drive her to the cabin. The very cabin she was found in. Neither of them knew how to get there.

They walked to the main lodge and ran into Nicki. She just had picked up coffee from the cafeteria. She put her coffee on the ground and grabbed Chloe giving her a giant hug. Nicki told her that she was going to head back to the operations center next to the cabin. She didn't have any updates on the boys or on Michelle. She waited near the cabin until it was well after dark. The deputy convinced her to head back to camp to try and rest. She reluctantly heeded his advice and using Michelle's truck she made her way back to Camp.

Chloe asked if she could get a ride back to the cabin with her.

"Are you kidding me, girl? No, you were airlifted yesterday, you can wait her. Rest up," answered Nicki. "If there is anything new, I will let you know. I promise."

Her father spoke up, "she can be rather convincing. Is it okay if we just follow you?"

Nick replied, "The roads are pretty rough for a car. Come on, I can't believe I am doing this."

The three got into Michelle's 4runner. Nicki drove them back to the cabin. It seemed like it was taking forever. They arrived just a few minutes before the sun rose. There didn't appear to be any clouds and the last of the remaining stars were beginning to extinguish out. Hopefully the weather cooperated so the search crews could get assistance from the air.

Nicki had no trouble finding the cabin again. There were police everywhere. The SUV with the flat tires had crime tape all around it. A cop sat on the metal chair guarding it. He was sipping on hot coffee. The morning was cold. Two generators, side by side, nearby were humming along. A large satellite dish was placed on the road.

There were no new updates. The search and rescue helicopter would be launching soon. They were also getting a state police helicopter to help in the search. The governor was also on her way to see if she could offer any additional help. She already stated that she would be willing to call up additional National Guard troops to assist in the search.

Everybody at the operations center seemed to know Chloe's father. They allowed him and his daughter into a large tent. Nicki came in a few minutes later. They were given seats along with hot drinks and pastries. They had maps taped against the wall. They even had computers up and going. Their monitors were the size of large screen televisions. One computer was showing the current weather in the region.

One gentleman, wearing a sweater that said "Mountain Rescue," came up and asked if they needed anything else. Chloe stood up and said she had to use the bathroom. She told her dad she would be right back. Nicki being overly protective offered to go with her, but Chloe politely told her no.

She bypassed the makeshift outhouses and wandered past the guarded SUV and towards the cabin. Besides the cop guarding the vehicle, everyone else was either in the tent or just outside it. Everyone was sipping on caffeine getting the needed energy to resume their search. She was by herself. She looked around to see if anyone was watching. She squatted down.

And there it was. The box. It was still there. She hid it yesterday when Nicki went to go flag down the police. It was extremely fortunate that Nicki left her by herself. Chloe was fatigued and incredibly sick yesterday so it took every ounce of her energy to get out of Michelle's truck and then spring open the back of the black SUV, grab the box, and carry it over. She was surprised how heavy it was. She didn't think she would be able to carry it very far. After the boys left, she thought about getting it then. She was too sick and she didn't know if those evil men were in the area. After placing the box, she hurried back. She saw the lights from the police truck and Nicki running so she decided to just lean up against the truck.

She first saw that box when she got in the back of the truck on Friday. It was covered by a towel, but she saw the corner of it peeking out. She only told Tyler about what she saw in the back of the truck.

Tyler told her that if anything should happen to him, he should get the brush from his locker. He didn't want anyone else finding it. He wrote down the combination to his locker and handed it to her.

She had covered the box with a bunch of limbs the day she took her first helicopter ride. It had been completely obscured. Now it wasn't as she removed all the dead wood from it. The black cat that sat on top of the box was absolutely stunning, it almost appeared as if the cat was looking up at her. She opened it up after some time of prying it open. She didn't have time the day before to look at it. There were two books in it and one was the journal written by Heffelfinger. It was like a journal she had never seen before. They sure don't make them like that anymore. The other one was a very thick book. It was extremely old. It looked like it was bounded in white and brown cracked leather. It had weird faded markings on it. She had her bag with her and she unrolled the brush. There was an empty pocket that was next to where the old text laid. She carefully placed it there as if she was putting down a sleeping newborn. She placed the journal on top and then she closed it. For the first time in a long time, she felt peaceful, like a soothing blanket had just been placed upon her shoulders. She put the box back in its hiding spot covering it back up. She didn't want anyone to accidentally stumble on upon it.

Looking around, she quickly walked back to the tent.

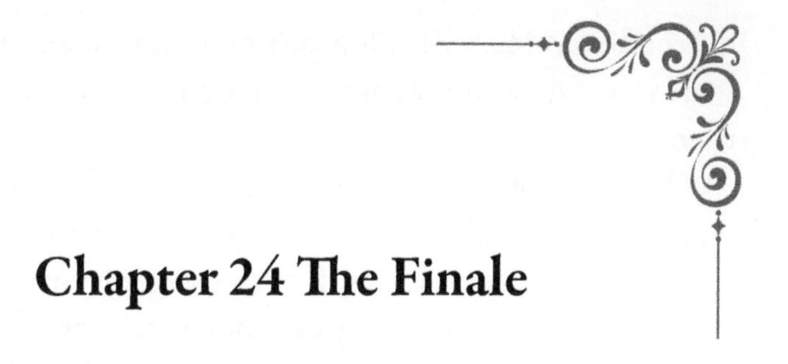

Chapter 24 The Finale

Nobody hardly slept the rest of the night out at the campfire. Lowland kept the fire going and kept a watchful eye on his three captives. He methodically added wood every time the fire threatened to die. Every so often, Alpine would yell at his brother and call him horrible names. He was very creative on the different derisive things he would say to his quiet brother. The tall man with the sleeve of tattoos had finally run out of words and insults and instead just stared at the fire with a look of disgust. A decade worth of work, for nothing. What a complete waste of time. He didn't care about the brush anymore. Without the cedar box, the brush was worthless. How would he get it anyhow. He just couldn't walk into camp or into Tyler's house and grab the thing. Just a dumb artifact. The only thing it did was stood the test of time and created turmoil for anyone dumb enough to look for it. Every so often he would angrily throw a rock into the fire just out of pure revulsion. The whole job he was paid to do was cursed from the beginning.

Tyler tried keeping his friend awake. He was afraid if he went to sleep, he might never wake up. Michelle dozed in and out. When she was awake, she would give words of encouragement to the boys. Tyler was at his limit, however, and so her words had little impact on his thoughts. He was beyond fatigued.

The sun finally rose and the three were still tied up to the tree. Jacob was still in and out of consciousness, despite his friend's best efforts to keep him awake. He was dehydrated and his broken arm only worsened his condition. Michelle still hadn't heard him speak. He was still in some sort of daze. This wasn't the same boy she met on the confidence course.

Alpine turned to his brother and told him it was time. There was no use putting it off. They needed to get out of the woods and back on the road to the Oregon Coast. They had to quickly make a plan on how they could get across the valley past the coastal range and into the port city without being apprehended by the authorities. Alpine had never missed his home country as he did now.

Tyler finally spoke up, "one thing, I have one question. Who hired you, was it Ethan Flynn?"

Alpine looked at Tyler and laughed, "no, I told ya, he had nutin' to do wit' it. It weren't who ya think."

Tyler was trying to extend the little time he had. He knew his fate. He knew their plans. He had nothing to lose. So, he asked, "so who then? I know you are going to kill us. I am not afraid. I look forward to seeing my mom. I will carry it to my grave. So, you might as well tell us." He looked up at Alpine with such vile hatred. His brown eyes bored into the tall man.

Alpine replied, "he was there, at the convention. He wanted to make sure we got the job done. Not sure if you remember him, Titans fan." Alpine glared back at Tyler, "Ha, ya do't have a Scooby do ya?"

Tyler as usual didn't comprehend half the man's vernacular. He wasn't quite sure what Scooby-Doo had to do with this whole affair. He was still trying to understand what a "sooty" was. Tyler wasn't lying to the evil man, he was actually looking forward to death, he was ready to sleep.

The man had nothing else to say to the captives. Alpine told his brother to finish the task at hand and then meet him at the trail. He admonished him not to screw this up, or he would kill him, family or not. They were going to stay on the trail heading downstream until they found a road. If they heard any helicopters they would duck into the forest.

Alpine didn't even look at the three that were bound to the tall evergreen. He spit on the ground with a sense of disgust and he just strolled back to the hiking trail as if he were on a weekend outing. He never turned around, not once.

About the time Chloe placed that brush into that cedar box, Alpine found his way back to the trail. It was a bit of walk back but he made it. He just got to the trail and heard the first shot. He stiffened. It was the last shot he heard, because he died right there on the hiking path. He went face first into the ground without so much as a murmur. His brother, Lowland, was behind him. He had stalked him the entire way. He knelt briefly next to him and wept. Standing up, he slowly lowered his pistol and put it back into his waistband.

Lowland quickly walked back to where the three captives were. They were still tied to the tree. Their heads hung low. He untied them. Even though it was still cool from the morning sunrise, he was sweating. His round face was redder than normal. He had tears streaming down his face.

"G'wed now, 'fore I change me mind. Never did like 'im." The short man walked off. It was the first and last words they heard that man say.

Tyler and Michelle stiffly stood up. Jacob slumped down. He was unconscious. Tyler and Michelle tried picking him up. They held him up the best they could and dragged the injured boy through the woods. They were careful not to further injure his arm. It seemed to take forever to get out of the thick forest. They were deeper in the woods than Michelle had estimated. They finally found the hiking trail. Then they heard the second shot of the day. That shot didn't startle them.

They saw Alpine lying there. He lay there with blood still seeping from his head. His eyes were still open. A look of surprise still painted on his ashen face. His cheek pressed against dead pine needles and wet duff.

They limped upstream and the two collapsed at once letting go of Jacob. They could go no further. Exhaustion and dehydration finally got the better of them. All three were face first on that fateful trail. Michelle lifted her heavy head and there in the distance she saw some sort of woman. She could not be sure. It looked like a female human body, her head adorned with a wide band that bore horns and stars. She had flowing black hair and dark eyes. She was wearing some sort of tan sheath dress that ran down to her sandaled feet. The dress had broad shoulder straps. She was tall and beautiful and she had long dark thin arms almost like a runway model. She was holding something in her right hand, almost like a painting brush. As she came closer, she saw it wasn't a goddess. It was a woman in uniform.

Epilogue

Michelle, Tyler, and Jacob were airlifted to a large hospital in Portland. They were all treated for dehydration and exposure. Michelle and Tyler were released the next morning. Jacob also suffered from shock, internal injuries, and a badly broken arm. They had to reset it. He stayed in the Portland hospital for a few additional days. Nicki, Michelle, and Jennifer never left his side.

Michelle and Nicki both received citizen medals from the Governor and the state police for their courageous, brave, and selfless actions in saving the four children of Camp Pertida. The authorities concluded that they went way above and beyond that would have been ever expected. The owners recognized their heroic actions and they subsequently put them in charge of managing and running Camp Pertida. After some new operating procedures were established and new training was conducted, the camp opened the following year. Nicki renamed Cabin B to honor Sirus Snodgrass. Real or not, that story would stay forever.

Ms. Betty Holstrom was never heard from since the day she was quietly escorted off the premises of Camp Pertida. Some say she retired early and moved to the East Coast with her four cats.

Jacob finally recovered from his injuries. It took the rest of the summer for him to fully heal from his ordeal. He never did go camping with his mother. Well, at least not that summer. They did hang out though. They watched plenty of movies and walked around their little town. They no longer kept secrets from each other and they took time to tell each other about their day. Jennifer started cooking dinner more for her son. Jennifer even made homemade pepperoni pizza sin mushroom. His mother went with him to counseling to work through his trauma and his anxiety. Jacob was a new kid. Michelle and Nicki made it a point to come and visit him at least once a month.

Ethan Flynn, having heard about his adventures, stopped by and brought Jacob a few signed movie posters. Jennifer thought he was pretty attractive. All three eventually went to his movie premier in Los Angeles. It was a movie about lost hikers and a brush. Jennifer wanted to know what could possibly be interesting about a hair brush.

Ryden's father was sent to jail for many years. The judge wasn't happy with his actions at the bar. The patron that had received the head injury had to go through a year of physical therapy. Plus, the judge suspected that he had physically abused his own son.

Ryden's aunt and uncle happily adopted him with a judge's approval. They weren't able to have children of their own. His new adopted parents lived in a little town of Scio. In fact, it's not too far from Jacob and Tyler. The three hung out almost every weekend. Ryden started an anti-bullying program at his new school.

Chloe's mother began teleworking and spent a lot of time with her daughter. Even Chloe's dad took more time off. They took a road trip to Anaheim and then they drove to the Grand Canyon. Chloe left her cell phone behind. They eventually spent every Friday night playing cards. No cell phones were ever allowed at the table. Chloe always kept in touch with her three best friends. She texted Jacob the most.

Lowland, the portly brother, was never found and neither was the gun. The brother's benefactor, the one who wanted the artifacts, was never identified, at least not by the authorities.

Tyler had the best luck of the four friends. It was never officially put on record how that box was eventually located. The box did find its way back to its rightful home. The Egyptian government safely and quietly stored their long-lost box into a hidden location. Even the journal written by Heffelfinger was sealed in the cedar box. The Egyptian officials felt it had every right to be in there as well. There was a copy supposedly made of Heffelfinger's journal and his adventure in Egypt, but that will be a story for another time.

The Egyptian Government was quite pleased the artifacts belonged in the correct country and as promised, they quietly rewarded the founder of their lost item. Tyler gave most of the money to his father. They even bought a new house. The new house was a block away from Jacob's. Much to the dismay of the old farmer, Jim quit his job and opened up a repair and body shop in Albany. He mostly restored muscle cars. He planned on giving his son a 1967 Mustang once he learned to drive. The business was extremely successful. He even hired two employees so he could spend more time with his son.

Tyler had enough money left over to buy a new pair of shoes and one comic book. He gave the comic book to his best friend.

THE END

Lightning Source UK Ltd.
Milton Keynes UK
UKHW010717131222
413853UK00001B/73

9 798215 425701